Dragons Within

Claiming Her Wings

Dragons Within

Claiming Her Wings

Balance of Seven
Dallas

Dragons Within
Claiming Her Wings

For information, contact:

Balance of Seven
www.balanceofseven.com
Publisher: ymalakova@balanceofseven.com
Managing Editor: dtinker@balanceofseven.com

Cover Design: Eben Schumacher Art
ebenschumacherart.artstation.com

Copyediting and Formatting: D Tinker Editing
www.balanceofseven.com/d-tinker-editing

French Language Consultant: C. M. Lander
German Language Consultant: D Tinker Editing

ISBN: 978-1-947012-80-6

Library of Congress Control Number: 2019946588

25 24 23 22 21 20 19 1 2 3 4 5

To those of you still seeking your dragon within:

may she give you wings to fly,

a voice to speak,

and fire to fight for what you believe in.

Contents

Introduction

Dear Readers, Dreamers, Humans, and Dragons,

Several years ago, I lived in a cave at the end of a long corridor. My throne was made of leather, I hoarded achievements like gold, but day after day, I drummed my fingers on my shiny mahogany desk.

I was restless, troubled. Ever since I'd made a commitment to finish the novel inside my head, I'd been dreaming of magic, dreaming of dragons. With each chapter I penned, the dreams came more and more frequently—but in the world I came from, magic wasn't real, and dragons were nothing more than the fancy of an eight-year-old boy.

I didn't truly know at the time that I was dreaming of dragons, because my dreams came to me in fragments—a flash here, a spark there. I could gaze only upon the eye of the dragon in them: glance at the deep, divine knowledge that my purpose in life was to do everything in my power to lift up words and art—both my own and others'—shining a light on all beautiful, soul-driven creations.

The very notion was overwhelming, at best; I didn't know what to do with it or if it was even possible. Some days, I snarled and breathed fire at the dreams. *Get real! Magic doesn't exist! Or if it does—I certainly don't have enough of it to help anyone.*

Over time, with support and encouragement from my friend and mentor, Debbie Burns, I gained the courage to trade the mahogany desk for one made of fairy-tale glass, and I partnered with a talented editor, Dorothy Tinker. Together, we began publishing speculative fiction books featuring new and emerging authors through our press, Balance of Seven. Last summer, our debut anthology became an instant #1 Amazon bestseller, and it has since become an award-winning publication, along with four more of our press's books.

As I embrace the role of both fiction writer and small press publisher, I have begun accumulating a new kind of treasure in my office: items inspired by our authors' creativity and my own artistry—a silver masquerade mask, an intrepid green flag attributed to General Corcoran's "Fighting Sixty-Ninth," a moonstone pendant, a pewter ouroboros bracelet . . .

The mask has come to represent my scales: that which keeps negative thoughts and cynicism from puncturing my dreams. The flag symbolizes my wings; I look to it on my worst days to keep forging forward without fear or regret. The moonstone holds the secrets of my inner magic: that which is unique to me. And the ouroboros signifies what I have become: I stopped being the woman who could only dream of dragons and became the one who makes them real.

It has truly been an honor working with the authors of this book, with Dorothy, and with our cover artist, Eben—sharing their passion, enthusiasm, and creativity. It's my hope that the unique stories in this collection inspire you to embrace your inner magic—and find your dragon within.

Ynes Malakova
CEO, Balance of Seven
Leader, Creative Central

Coronation by Blood

C. M. Lander

On the day Rhaeynn hatched from her infinitesimal shell, a dream wrested the postnatal sleep of her mother, Mayghylos. A badly injured human marched haltingly through a burning valley. Ash and blood adorned her bright white flesh. Slashes of fabric that once might have been leather armor clung desperately to her form. It was night, and smoke was thick, but it did not choke the woman. She was used to fire; it gave her life.

Mayghylos watched helplessly, a spear pinning her massive wings to the ground, as the woman walked past her. Night seemed to crowd out the flames, and a figure formed of shadow began to speak, its thin silver outline standing head and shoulders above the small woman.

"Ah, the fire bringer. At last we meet. Such a pity it should be at your end."

"Ze'Nato." The word sounded like a curse coming from her spitting lips. A word Mayghylos had not heard now for eons. A word lost to the centuries for the speakers of the ancient tongue. The only word that could strike fear in the dragon queen's heart.

The First Night.

Startled from her slumber, Mayghylos looked to her drakeling. Her flesh was pink and had not yet formed scales. The hatchling was small, barely the size of her mother's talon, and Mayghylos feared she would not last the night. Awake now, the dragon mother nestled close to her shivering offspring. The heat from her mother's maw radiated through Rhaeynn's tender flesh. Ze'Nato was a bad omen for her to dream of on her last child's first night. The mother laid her head upon the nest of feathers and twigs she had built at the mouth of her volcanic home and shed a silent tear for her young, mourning her loss before it even came.

At 622 years of age, Rhaeynn remained the youngest of Mayghylos's offspring. The runt of the horde, her peach flesh had never ripened into jewel-toned scales as her brothers' had. She was soft, with opalescent shimmers covering her arms and hind legs that acted more as decoration than armor. Her snout did not protrude with a long, toothy jaw, as the snout of any dragon before her had. Rather, her face—for that was the only word for it—was smooth and round. Her teeth, though jagged, were housed in a mouth too small to rend oxen limb from limb. Her cheeks rounded into a tiny southern peak of a jaw. The only plate about her was the plait of hair that terminated just shy of her waist: its blonde entirety dappled with shades of pink and purple.

Most curious of all, though, was her lack of wings or tail. Each dragon before her had one or the other, if not both. But she was utterly without. She appeared, to the few who ever saw her, to be more human than dragon: a portent that the prophecy of Mayghylos's dream from Rhaeynn's birthnight was soon to be fulfilled.

So Mayghylos had hidden her away from the violent world.

She lived in her mother's den, protected perpetually by the volcano's molten base, even when, on the rare occasion, her mother went out to stretch her wings. Set in a cavern toward the tip of the mountain, Rhaeynn lived among her hoard: a library of books obtained over the decades from her dearest friend and only tie to the outside world, Offram.

Offram was the Envoy of the Sacred Accords, a human mage—one of the few still remaining—and the only human permitted within the dragon realm of the Northlands. He oversaw the peaceful coexistence of dragons and humans, as agreed upon by the dragon queen, Mayghylos, and his own queen, Umara, after years of death on both sides. He spoke both the ancient tongue of magic, which bound all life together in the beginning, and the common tongue, now used by humans to communicate with each other, and he taught Rhaeynn the words of the common tongue so she might read more.

Offram had discovered Rhaeynn quite by accident as the little drake had grown curious about this visitor who seemed more like herself than her own mother. Unable to silence the man for good for fear of starting another war, Mayghylos pleaded with Offram to keep her daughter's life a secret. And he did. For he had found within the dragon princess an innocence so profound, he could not steal it from the world. Her violet eyes burned with such curiosity that he wished a curse on any who would dare extinguish them.

Within the pages of her treasured tomes, Rhaeynn found a piece of herself. A familiarity with the shapes. For a very long time, she even wondered if Offram might have been her father, but she was far older than him. His existence was but a twinkle in her years. She noted how her friend's face turned from taut to wrinkled, his hair from black to white, his sparkling eyes now sunken. Time took its toll on Offram and, in turn, took Offram himself.

As the queen of dragons, Mayghylos had to keep up appearances for her millennial reign, so she built a golden chamber filled with treasures from around the world. Gifts from ancient civilizations, from a time when magical beings coexisted—a time before humans. Golden columns stacked with coins and jewels and treasures flickered from within the volcano's belly each time the queen took a breath in its main chamber.

However, gold was not Mayghylos's preferred hoard. Within her private chambers, nearest the top of their familial mount, Mayghylos resided among a collection of flowers: a cave of green and red and purple, pink and lavender that grew toward the opening in the wall through which sunlight poured. Garlands of white lilies and golden poms meandered their way around the cavern's ceiling. Inside her cave, her purple ombré scales blended in like shining petals. The dragon queen loved life more than anything. More than gold.

And it was through that sunlit portal that Mayghylos would gaze at the island just east of her kingdom.

Before the signing of the Sacred Accords, dragons were free to wander wherever they pleased. Magic had existed in all beings and murder had not been known within the realm of light. But one day, a darkness took hold of the lands and the plentiful life the world had known was gone. Magic fought magic for resources, for life. And humans were born where the magical resources were depleted.

"The poor humans," Mayghylos had once told Rhaeynn. "They never knew a world without battle. Without war. This is not the way of our world. The true way knows only one path: peace."

Humans had seemed like mystical beasts before Rhaeynn found her books. Now, as she traced their round faces in her books and laid hands upon her own cheeks, she wondered how weak she was compared to her great mother.

Rhaeynn made her way up the side of her mountainous home, pulling herself up nimbly with barely an effort expended. She nestled herself within a thicket of wildflowers at the mouth of Mayghylos's cave; her mother had brought them in only the day before. The dragon queen was out for a scouting flight with her eldest son, the blue-scaled Za'dreth. Her middle son, Denoth, had stayed behind to guard the den and Rhaeynn. The family had become restless. Offram had been missing for some months now, and the winds spoke of danger in the southern kingdom. Of the death of magic. Of a building army.

Denoth hated his little sister. "The result of my mother's tryst with some ancient wizard, long gone," he'd say to the wind and the trees in frequent moments of annoyance with the curious sprite that was Rhaeynn. "The dragon who cannot fly," he'd jeer. "Worse than a wyrm."

Only once did his words affect the young drake. She had

retreated to her mother's chambers and sobbed her anguish into a cluster of clover.

"My dear Rhaeynn," Mayghylos had comforted, "I alone created you from the well of my precious magic in the hope that you might carry on the dragon line. We great beasts of wing are not long for this world. Fearsome though we may be, the humans have always found a reason and a way to hunt us. But you, daughter, are our savior. You are small and can blend in with the humans. Learn their plans and play them against each other. You, daughter, will outlive us all. And you alone will save our kind."

The words played in Rhaeynn's mind whenever she heard Denoth's barbs. She found strength in them.

As Rhaeynn lounged among the flowers, enjoying their fertile fragrances, protective spells jingled their warning in her ears. She looked due south from her mother's lair to the only entrance into the dragon's realm: a clearing in the thick green forest that surrounded the fields of mossy black rock leading up to their volcanic home.

For a fleeting moment, she tried to conjure Offram, striding happily through the forest wall in his aged way, joyful and unaware of his lateness. But she knew that could not be. There were intruders at the gate. Death had come for the last of the dragons.

A signal bleated its way through the trees when, finally, the first of a parade of humans marched their way into the restricted lands, their armor glinting in the sunlight. Rhaeynn had never seen quite so many small creatures moving in formation, save the birds that made their migrations without hesitation over the ancient mount. The birds knew they were safe among the dragons, but the humans had never warmed to the enormous winged diplomats.

The humans' banners burned a deep red, with a faint black outline she couldn't quite make out until they were halfway up the obsidian plaza: a dragon with a golden spear through its chest. These were not the colors of the human queen Umara of Anondale, who had established peace between the humans and the dragons. Her banners were a deep blue that calmed Rhaeynn each time she saw Offram arriving in a tunic the color of the sea.

These humans brought with them spears, archers, and swords. Oxen dragged a large contraption that Rhaeynn had read of in a book: a mangonel. The lumbering honey-hued timbers stretched the length of six rows of soldiers. Its enormous arm stood poised. From her perch at the opening of her mother's cave, Rhaeynn could hear the ropes pulling the arm tight against the mangonel's base. As the soldiers came to a halt, four men scrambled to the end of the arm to load a swollen bladder ball into the well of the weapon.

"Mayghylos!" shouted a man seated atop a white horse in the front line. His voice was deep with false bravado. He had refused to wear a helmet, while his men were all suited to the teeth. His golden hair shimmered in the sunlight. Rhaeynn caught her first whiff of human pretension, and it smelled much like Denoth.

"Mayghylos," the man repeated. "Your reign is ended." He scoped the sky above his head as his soldiers crowded around him, shields held up at an angle to protect against any raining fire they might encounter should the dragon queen approach.

A silence came over the land as the man awaited a reply. Rhaeynn held her breath. She studied the faces of the men beneath: steadfast and angry. Hateful monsters she had never dreamed could exist. The history texts spoke of battles and war but never in this visceral detail.

She clenched her jaw, stifling a need to call out for her mother. Her sheltered life was suddenly crumbling around her at once. She had never hunted before. Offram's duties had included driving oxen to the dragon's lair to ensure they were fed and would never feast upon any other animal. It was a tiring diet, but one she had understood the necessity of.

With no Offram to bring them food, the dragons had recently settled for scavenging, but their bellies had growled with a need that awakened ancient urges within them. Rhaeynn could feel her fingers tightening against her flesh, her talons drawing blood she did not notice. The muscles in her back flexed as she fought the impulse to fly from her hiding place and eviscerate the men where they stood. This was not her war. Not yet.

Darkness clouded over them as if the sun had flickered. The men looked to one another, unsure of how to position themselves, when from the sky sounded a great tritonal shrieking, followed by a massive whip of wind and wing as a blue haze of scale and tail soared past, diving at the army and breathing terrible flames upon it.

It was Za'dreth, back from his scouting mission earlier than expected. As he finished his first pass, he turned around. His body was too large to be lithe, but he still managed to attack again before the men could regroup. Screams flooded the air. The scent of brimstone and burning flesh filled Rhaeynn's nostrils like a welcome holiday roast. She felt an excitement yet unknown to her rise within her body and licked her lips with desire. She steadied herself upon the ledge, ready to fling herself down the mountain as she had run so many times as an innocent girl.

Now she would throw herself into battle.

The sound of horse hooves over the fray froze Rhaeynn in her place. She watched, an unknown sentinel, as the leader of the army rode his way to the back of the mangonel. Bypassing burning men who pleaded for his aid, the leader raised his sword and dropped it upon the tenuous rope there, which snapped with great relief beneath the pressure of his blade.

The bulbous bladder flew through the air and struck Za'dreth midflight. Limpid liquid coated him as he cried out in agony. In Rhaeynn's short centuries of life, she had never known her brother to even register pain. In the recent past, just before the Sacred Accords, whenever young knights chose him as a target to prove their valor, he had never so much as winced when a spear caught his underbelly. He had merely exhaled his annoyance in a stream of flames that fried the former knights to blackened crisps. She could still remember the taste of charred knight, sneaked hastily as a treat behind her mother's back, from her childhood.

Za'dreth dropped to the ground, his body trenching the rocky field beneath him. Bits of rubble flew into the air and pummeled the burning soldiers as they writhed on the ground.

From her vantage, Rhaeynn could see Za'dreth's scales sizzling as the plates deteriorated to nothing and the black ooze of dragon blood pooled just below him. The serum had penetrated his defenses and eaten him alive. She wanted to cry out. To scream. To shout her primal war cry and rush down the mountain, finishing off the men who remained and avenging her brother.

But the sun went out again.

Mayghylos had returned.

Her massive wingspan blotted out the sun for far longer than her son's. She floated down to the ground, the world shaking as her hind legs made contact. Her body shone deep purple with hints of lilac at the tips of each domed scale. When she reared to stand at her full height, she was almost half the size of the volcano itself. Rhaeynn had never noticed how much her mother stooped to stay hidden within their walls. The Northlands were too small a place for such massive creatures to be kept. The kingdom of rock and ash, which had once seemed so expansive to Rhaeynn, was now dwarfed by her mother's enormity.

This was no place for dragons.

Rhaeynn realized in that moment what her family had given up in the Sacred Accords to allay the fears of the humans. To make them feel comfortable in their own lands. But never once had the humans cared to realize the punishment their comfort imposed upon the dragons. Rage coursed through her vibrating body, along with satisfaction at her mother's return. Revenge would be had.

"Mayghylos," the blond man called out from beside the well of the mangonel as the few remaining men scrambled to lift another bladder into the weapon. Their clothing burned and smoked, and with each movement, they winced in pain. This pleased Rhaeynn immensely.

"I am Mayghylos, Queen of the Northlands and sovereign of all magic. You have trespassed upon my kingdom and murdered my son, the prince Za'dreth. Tell me quickly who I shall inform Queen Umara I am killing." Her voice resonated throughout the valley with an intensity that shook the ground for miles.

The blond man gave a smug smile. "Queen Umara is dead. And you have breached your obligations under the Sacred Accords in creating a weapon with which to defeat mankind."

They knew she was there. They knew she existed.

"I am Jakkir, second son of King Felrick, sent to administer your punishment."

"You are nothing and no one!" Mayghylos roared. "And I do not recognize your father as the leader of man. The winds tell me he is a usurper and an inciter. And you, his second son . . ."

The bile behind her voice sent Rhaeynn's gaze to the cave in the neighboring mountain, where Denoth cowered, looking on at their brother's demise with not an inkling of anger. Only fear and a betrayal of what all dragonkind stood for.

"You have no authority, you puny little man."

A ball of fire grew within Mayghylos's throat as she prepared to end the war once and for all. But as her words filled the valley once more, the sound was clipped by Jakkir's sword falling upon a taut rope and snapping the bladder of venom at Mayghylos.

The queen screamed in anger and fell beside her fallen son. Her eyes fluttered as his corpse fell in and out of view, blurring in a blue haze. She nuzzled her snout against the crook of his talon with the last of her strength, a final goodbye to the world she loved.

It happened so fast. So much faster than Rhaeynn could have imagined. Her mother fell in an instant. The acid burned holes in her armor and ate through her flesh, as it had her brother just moments before.

Tears clung to Rhaeynn's eyes as she watched her mother writhe in pain. She could not contain herself. She screeched, giving away her location as she ran down the face of the mountain at full speed. She could not think in that moment. Rage blinded her to the foolishness of her actions. If the soldiers could destroy the two largest dragons in the world, what chance did she stand, with her soft pink flesh? But she would not be deterred. She barreled toward Jakkir as his remaining soldiers reloaded the mangonel once more.

She heard nothing but the beating of her feet against the ground. She saw nothing but Jakkir's pale face smirking with pleasure at her pain. She felt nothing but the constant, quick beat of her heart bidding her forward. She crushed the bones of fallen soldiers beneath her dirt-clouded feet as she raced her way forward, but her foot caught on a half-melted shield and she fell to the ground.

Jakkir dismounted and strode toward Rhaeynn before she could stand again, holding his sword to her neck. The same sword that had killed her mother and brother. She rose, pressing her neck against the blade's tip.

"I am Rhaeynn, princess of the Northlands, born of Mayghylos's might. I will drink your blood and your venom, and you will know me as queen of all the land. I will avenge my mother and my kind, and you, Jakkir, will burn."

Jakkir lifted one eyebrow as he tightened his muscles to push the blade through Rhaeynn's neck, but he found no strength left in his arm. He was frozen, unable to move of his own accord. For the first time, fear flashed across his face, but all he could move were his eyes as they darted around, seeking help.

The three soldiers who had loaded the mangonel ran for cover, desperately seeking the opening in the forest that would take them back to the road. A road they would never make it to. Rhaeynn narrowed her eyes, and in an instant, all three men's necks snapped. Their bodies fell limp to the ground.

Jakkir watched their deaths helplessly. Sweat beaded his brow. His breath caught in his chest. He wanted to plead for clemency, but he could not find the strength to speak.

"You don't deserve the mercy of a snapped neck," Rhaeynn told him. "No, you deserve something special, second son of Felrick."

A smile broke over Rhaeynn's face as the mangonel moved into position on its own. She stepped back, savoring the look on Jakkir's face as the reality of his situation set in. He would have screamed if he could. He would have cried like a child for his father to save him, but Rhaeynn wouldn't afford him such relief.

"You are nothing and no one."

As Rhaeynn repeated her mother's words, the rope snapped and the bladder struck Jakkir, its thin membrane rupturing. The acid devoured him entirely. There was not a single blond strand left of the second son of Felrick.

Rhaeynn surveyed her homeland. Corpses littered the mountain face. She waved her hand, and the bodies of the humans disappeared. Only Mayghylos and Za'dreth remained.

She approached her brother with a soothing deference that defied the rage within her. She laid a hand on his snout, touching his blue-black jowl.

"Of fire I am. To fire I shall return."

His body erupted in flames that burned blue until he was entirely consumed. The flames went completely yellow, then they burned white and disappeared entirely. Rhaeynn took a moment to breathe her goodbye to her brother before shifting to her mother.

She knelt at Mayghylos's head and held her mother close. Tears fell down her opalescent cheeks as she kissed her mother for the last time. "Of fire I am. To fire I shall return."

In a flash of lavender flame, Mayghylos was gone.

The humans would pay. Their time leading the world had come to an end in Rhaeynn's eyes. Their civilizations would crumble, and the world would return to the true way: one of peace and magical supremacy.

A flutter of wings drew her from her scheming. Denoth. Her cowardly brother had hidden throughout the battle and refused to aid his mother in her time of need. Rhaeynn watched as Denoth flew away from their home in the Northlands without a single word.

With Denoth abandoning their home, Rhaeynn would rule as queen. She would build an army of magic to fight alongside her. She would rule wholly and reclaim the status that magic had once held in the world.

And she would do to humans what they had done to the magical beings of the realm since their genesis: enslave them all.

Drachenpferde

JT Morse

In a clearing just beyond the western edge of the Black Forest, I saw them. Sleek and magnificent, they were bridled with mystery. That was where I first witnessed their mythical power. What I would come to know as our power.

At the tender age of three, I fell in love with horses. The nuzzle of a gentle giant's nose, whisking a teardrop from my cheek, changed me forever. Clyde was the first, but he certainly was not the last equine connection I've made in my twenty-two years of life. Nothing else in this entire world has enraptured my heart or captivated me the way horses do. Books and reading come close, but they're still not as "me" as horses are. I have no doubt that *Equus caballus* is my spirit animal. Over the years, I've even toyed with the idea that I might be part horse.

It took a friend nearly dying and a trip halfway around the world for me to realize how close to the truth I was with that off-the-cuff contemplation.

Last May, less than a week after I'd graduated with a bachelor's in biology—headed toward a master's and a career in the field of large animal veterinary medicine—I received The Call from Anna.

Yes, this call fell into the category of *the* with a capital *T* and *call* with a capital *C*. My precious soul sister of over a decade had been diagnosed a few months prior with ALL, acute lymphocytic leukemia. She'd waited to call me until all the tests had come back and they'd given her an idea of how long—well, you know.

As anyone could guess, I fell apart as soon as we hung up, devastated. Anna and I had been besties since sixth grade. She'd never missed any of my riding competitions, and I'd never missed any of her performances—which meant that by the time she left to join a ballet company in Germany at twenty, I'd seen *The Nutcracker* thirty-eight times. No lie. But to be honest, I'd have watched it another thirty-eight million if it could have saved her.

Before she broke the news about her illness, Anna had tried to convince me to come visit her by tantalizing me with a legend of creatures called *Drachenpferde*. That girl knew me too well; she knew that anything having to do with horses—and dragons, for that matter—would pique my interest and should have been enough to get me on a plane.

However, I didn't take the bait; I had too much on my plate prepping for my upcoming summer internship at an equine hospital in Waller. She had to come clean and break the bad news before I would drop everything and run to the airport to catch the next flight to Berlin.

The S-Bahn ride from the airport to her apartment took an eternity. As I stood outside her building, the weight and gravity of the situation brought me to my emotional knees. I couldn't hold back the tsunami of tears that I'd been bravely holding back all the way from Houston, Texas, to Berlin, Germany.

I pawed at my face, smacking at wet cheeks with my hands until they blindly found the horse pendant hanging from a leather strap around my neck. I clutched at it as if it could save me from this moment. Save Anna from this moment. Save us from this horrific moment.

I ran my thumb across its smooth silvery mane like I'd done a thousand times before. But this time, it wasn't for good luck on a test or for reassurance as I climbed into the saddle of a green broke horse. This time, I needed it to save the one who'd given it to me for my sixteenth birthday. I needed it to save my Anna.

"You planning to come in anytime soon, Jen? Or had you planned to sleep out here on the sidewalk?"

Looking up through saltwater laced with fear, guilt, and abject terror, I saw her. Her body was thinner than her usual petite but ballet-strong proportions, she had bluish bags under her eyes, and her normally shiny black hair hung limp and dull. But her smile was all her. A smile that even from across the ocean could usually calm my fears and wash away any inklings of self-doubt.

"Come here, silly filly." Her open arms looked like salvation, and her eyes sang of the purest form of universal love.

"I'm so sorry. I'm supposed to be the pillar of strength here, and—"

"Hush, hush." She pulled me to her. "You came. That's all I needed. Anything else will be strawberry icing on a lemon cake."

"You know that's the weirdest flavor combo for a dessert, right?"

"And since when is being weird a crime?" Pulling slightly back from our embrace, Anna raised a sparse eyebrow.

I shrugged—my only response, since the tears had started to gush again.

"Come on, Jenny Whinny. You smell ever so slightly of horse manure mixed with sweat and a hint of hot rubber. Did you do a conveyor-belt rodeo at the luggage pickup when you arrived?"

My sobs turned to laughs. "No, I haven't done that in forever."

"Don't lie. I'm your Anna. I know things." She handed me a tissue, then started to gather my scattered bags. "Like the fact you did your signature luggage rodeo two summers ago when we went to that international bareback championship thingy in Mexico City."

I blew my nose with one hand and reached out with the other to take my heaviest bag from her.

She elbowed me in the ribs. "The championship that someone I know won."

"Yeah, yeah. So I can ride horses. Big deal."

"Oh, girl. You don't ride horses; you R-I-D-E them."

"That's gross, Anna."

"I didn't mean it like that!"

We both burst into uncontrollable laughter as we made our way into the stocky brick building and up a short flight of stairs to her apartment. I'd only been there once before, but it felt like home. The amazing evening melted into a mix of humorous memories, in-person retellings of stories we'd shared via email, and lots of tissues. We fell asleep wrapped in each other's arms, lying half-in and half-out of the cushion/pillow/afghan fort we'd built for old times' sake. Due to utter exhaustion, I slept like a newborn foal.

The next few days were a whirlwind of escorting Anna to doctor's visits, learning the local S- and U-Bahn schedules, and making the necessary arrangements to stay as long as I could. Life back in Texas would have to be put on hold for a bit.

For Anna, the hassle was worth it.

Late afternoon on day six, after tucking Anna in for her post-treatment snooze, I decided to head to the closest *Staatsbibliothek* to see if I could snag some books about the legend of the *Drachenpferde* that Anna had mentioned during The Call. I needed something to focus on, other than leukemia and death. I'd had enough of those.

Although there wasn't a plethora of options, the librarian showed me to the section on German mythology, and I found two books—printed in English, thank goodness—that mentioned these mythological dragon-horses. I checked the books out with Anna's ID number—no one even questioned me! I guess, with this being a college town like my own back home, the library staff were used to foreign students and such. Or maybe Germans were more trusting than Texans. Who knows? Bottom line is, I got the books and went back to the apartment to read.

Between my online searches and the books—I do love the smell of paper and leather bindings—I didn't learn a ton. But there was one article I found posted on a website that said there had been a sighting of these illusive dragon-horse hybrids near the Black Forest, close to the border between Germany and France.

When Anna woke on day twelve of my stay, I hit her with a proposal.

"Um, now that you've somewhat recovered from your treatment and you don't have another one scheduled for a week, how do you feel about us taking a road trip?" I tried to look as sweet and suppliant as possible.

She grinned. "And where is it that my adventurous friend would like to go? I'm not sure I'm up for the Eiffel Tower or Rome."

"No. I wasn't even thinking of leaving this country. Just a nice, little jaunt down to a town called Freiburg. Rumor has it, there are four monasteries in that one town. I know how you love getting back to your Catholic roots and touching history."

"Uh-huh. What's in it for you, filly girl?"

I threw my hands up and stuck out my lip. "Why would there have to be anything for me? I simply thought it would be nice to get my sick friend out of her stuffy apartment and whisk her off to go see some nuns and monks and old churchy architecture."

Anna didn't say anything. Instead, she walked over casually and put her forehead to mine. We both instinctually closed our eyes as our breathing fell into rhythm—a personal ritual we'd done for years.

"Okay, okay. No need to do your mind meld thing with me. You're right; I have an ulterior motive."

"I don't care. It doesn't matter. I'd love to go to Freiburg with you for a day or two."

"Really?

"Really. Absolutely. And with every fiber of my being."

"I love you, so much. You know that, right?"

"You dropped everything and came to be with me when I needed you most. Yeah, I know. And I love you too. Hence why I'm willing to go on this grandiose adventure with you."

"Don't you want to know my ulterior motive?"

Anna shook her head and walked into the kitchen to make a pot of lavender oolong.

We were going to Freiburg! Her, to see devout Christians and to commune with something bigger than herself. Me, to hunt for mythological dragon-horses. This was normal for us. A perfect and typical Anna-Jen journey.

I was so hyped from the train ride—which I've always found magical and exciting—that after we checked into the bed and breakfast, I mentioned I might go exploring. Anna said she was tired from the trip anyway and agreed that taking a nap would be easier if I wasn't bouncing off the ivy-wallpapered walls. Without hesitation, I plotted a course via street train, a kind taxi driver, and a short hike to get me to the latitude and longitude mentioned in the online article.

Thank goodness for the compass app on my phone!

Only a smidge over an hour later, I stood at the western edge of the ancient forest, peering into a clearing about the size of a standard dressage arena—a hundred feet across by two hundred feet long. The sun was making its way toward slumber as the moon began to rise, casting a transitional glow onto the empty meadow. Dapples of orange and yellow danced with silvery purple shadows.

I smiled. Despite being all alone in a forest made famous by dark fairy tales, I felt safe. Maybe the safest I'd ever felt, except for when I was in Anna's arms.

Nestled into a recliner of sorts that I'd fashioned out of a downed pine tree and my backpack, I watched the sun say its final good night and the man in the moon take over the sky. Pulling a granola bar from a side pocket of my pack, I decided I'd give these *Drachenpferde* two hours to make an appearance before I headed back to Anna.

Barely one bite into my cinnamon-laced snack, I noticed a flash of dark movement on the far side of the clearing. The fullness of the moon and the cloudless night sky offered a fair bit of light for me to see by, but the movement was happening in the shadows of the mighty oaks guarding the meadow. Under their branches, I could just make out the silhouette of—

Horses! A herd of about ten or twelve lean horses, each fifteen to seventeen hands tall. I stood and dropped the granola bar on top of my pack. I waffled between trying to stand perfectly still—so as not to spook them—and wanting to run across the field at top speed for a closer look. Luckily, staying put won out; I don't know if I could have seen what I saw next had I scared them away.

A few at a time, the mysterious horses stepped out of the arboreal shadows. As the moonlight draped and dressed them, their true nature revealed itself. Instead of the fur and hair I'd expected to see covering their bodies, they had scales—like those on fish but bigger. In the reflected and refracted light, their skin looked iridescent. Each horse—or rather *Drachenpferd*, as I had no doubt that's what these were—was a different color. Some of their scales were shades of red and purple; others radiated blues and greens. One stood slightly apart from the others and bore scales that were a wraithlike blend of white and silver.

Terrified to even breathe or blink, I stood as frozen as possible. However, as I did, part of me desperately screamed for me to pull out my phone and take as many pictures as possible. No one would ever believe this.

Except Anna. She would believe me, with proof or without.

As soon as my ailing bestie came to mind, the white dragon-horse raised its head and unfurled the biggest wings I'd ever seen or imagined on any creature, living or fictional. Unlike the wings of dragons in most movies and TV shows, these weren't bat-like. Nor were they feathered, like those of a bird. Instead, they were almost transparent. Ethereal. As if I were seeing them through a pane of wet glass on a chilly day. While their bodies seemed solid and defined, the wings they all began unfurling were the opposite; they were intangible and elusive.

Distracted as I watched the incredible display unfolding before me, I didn't notice that the white one had started walking toward me.

It halted a few feet away and exhaled audibly. Not a snort of concern or warning, but more an exhalation of peace. Although, I'm still not sure which of us the breath was meant to help calm. I daresay I might have needed it more at the time.

Turning my head ever so slowly, I blinked a few times against the radiance of its moonlit scales and wings. Without word or request on my part—I couldn't have uttered a word in that moment if I'd wanted to—the creature lowered its head toward me as if in invitation. I reached out with a trembling hand. When fingertips met scales, a ripple spread, from the place I'd touched between its ears, throughout and down its glowing body. A human pebble being dropped into a *Drachenpferd* pond. I jerked my hand back, fearing I'd hurt it—like a salty, sweaty touch to a slug in the summer.

The beautiful being gave a full-body shiver. Then, instead of retreating as I'd expected it to, it stepped toward me and nuzzled its massive head into my shoulder—such a simple but powerful gesture. I'd only experienced similar sensations twice in my lifetime. Once with Clyde, sweet old draft horse that he'd been, and once with Misty, the Arabian with whom I'd won more competitions than any other horse I'd ever trained or competed with. Sadly, she'd passed away about a year prior to this encounter, and I hadn't been on a horse since. I just couldn't.

I'd seen so much death and sickness in the past twelve months—Misty, my mom, and now Anna. As I began to get sucked down into the spiral of self-pity and sadness, I sensed something else on the periphery of my anguish. Something warm and tender. Something I desperately needed. With eyes closed and heart hurting, I felt a nuzzle whisk a teardrop from my cheek.

As I opened my eyes, the *Drachenpferd* raised its head, bringing us eye-to-eye. I became entranced by the depths of those dark brown, almost black, pools of love. Instantly, I knew her. Yes, her. Somehow, I was aware that Albieta was, in fact, a she. As well, I knew that this was where I was meant to be, that those magnificent creatures held a secret I needed in order to save myself and my best friend.

In unison, the rest of the herd encircled us, lifting their heads toward the stars and shooting flames into the star-sprinkled sky. As they did, Albieta knelt on her front legs, and without hesitation, I climbed aboard. What happened next could have come straight out of any dragon story I'd read as a kid.

We flew—across the dew-kissed field and above the treetops. But it wasn't only my body that raced and soared with the dragon-horses; my heart felt lighter than it had in years, and my mind opened to possibilities beyond fantasy and science fiction. During our flight, Albieta imparted to me a secret: I had the power to cure Anna. Deep inside me slept the essence of the *Drachenpferde*, the mystical ability to love unconditionally and to heal—myself and others.

Evidently, there are a handful of humans with the gift of *Pferdesprechen*, a mystical horse-whisperer-like quality. Those with the gift are obsessive horse-lovers with huge hearts and an unearthly sense of devotion to those we love. During that incredible night, I learned who I was—at my core, in my essence. Then, before the sun rose, I returned to Freiburg with a story beyond most people's belief and a bit of miraculous, life-saving news for my Anna.

Over the past six months, I've used my *Drachenpferd* talents to save not only Anna but also a dozen others with life-threatening maladies. Do I consider myself special or gifted? No. But I do consider myself blessed and fortunate.

So far, my secret has been kept by those I've healed and their loved ones. Someday, though, I'm sure I'll be outed and will have to devise a way to deal with the situation or simply disappear. For now, I relish the gift I've been given, and I love everyone I meet with the expansive love I discovered in a meadow on the edge of the Black Forest.

Of Blood and Scales

A. R. Coble

In the cool, crisp night air, gooseflesh covered the areas of my arms not covered in scales. Around me, my fellow magi, Draconians capable of magic, trudged toward reprieve after being driven from their home. Our home.

Camelot.

Physically, we magi looked like any other Draconians. Magically, we radiated an aura that nonmagical Draconians could not see, a distinction that bred fear among the nonmagical. A fear that was not eased by the fact that nonmagical Draconians could give birth to magi, and vice versa. A fear that my own nonmagical brother, Arthur, had taken advantage of mere hours ago to call for my death and usurp my throne.

Underestimating me, he believed me dead. He was always underestimating his big sister.

"Is Queen Morgana really dead, Mummy?" My skin prickled anew; the child was speaking of *me.*

"Yes, love. I'm afraid so," the child's mother answered softly.

"Who will keep us safe?"

My dual hearts burned as they sank into the pit of my stomach. Who *would* keep them safe? I had to maintain the appearance that I was dead, or Arthur would hunt down every last magus and murder them. Even the children.

"I don't know, darling. Sleep now." The mother smoothed a hand over the back of the inquisitive child in her arms. The despair in her voice created an aching hole in my chest.

As the trek continued, I began to wonder about my guard. Had any of them survived? Lancelot, Gawain, and Kay had served my parents before me. They were loyal and deserved so much better than to be cut down by a traitor.

Just as the sun rose bright and golden on the eastern side of Dozmary Pool, we came to a halt.

"Those who are able will set up camp. The rest will tend to each other and help with the children." Guinevere, my general, didn't sound even slightly tired. She led this group of refugees, and she alone knew that I was among the crowd.

I approached her warily, as someone might if they were not familiar with her. "What would you have me do, General?" My voice was disguised as well, but Guinevere had been present when I applied the glamour.

She eyed me. To anyone else, it would seem like she was scrutinizing, taking stock of my condition. It was a well-played response to my ruse of being a tired, old woman.

"You may gather wood for a fire. Don't stray too far, and yell if you need help. No magic, unless it is an extreme emergency. Understood?"

I smiled at my general, grateful for the opportunity to be useful and blend in. "Yes, General. Thank you."

I took off into the woods, heeding Guinevere's warnings and guidelines. Well, mostly. She had said no magic, but I needed something for hauling the wood back to camp, so I conjured a stretcher that I could load and easily drag behind me.

I was nearly finished loading the wood onto the stretcher when I heard a rustling in the leaves behind me. Whirling around, I found a man standing there.

My instincts screamed *danger*, but one look in his eyes told me he was no threat to me. His dark, corded hair and magnificently orange eyes revealed a soft creature, not one prone to violence. Covered in scales in all the usual places—jawline, outer arms, and elbows—he had the most magnificent aura of any magus I'd ever seen.

"Your Majesty, it isn't safe for you to be in the woods on your own."

I took a startled step backward. Nobody knew I was here. I was presumed dead.

"Forgive me, Your Majesty," he said, bowing his head in respect. "I can see through your glamour."

"Who are you?" I spoke carefully to prevent my fear from saturating my tone. Though if he could see through my glamour, he could probably see through my tone of voice as well.

"I am Merlin."

Merlin. There wasn't a soul alive who hadn't heard of Merlin. He had a reputation as a hermit and the greatest sorcerer in Draconian history.

"I'm known to be dead," was my intelligent reply.

"What shall I call you, then?" A sweet smile turned up the corners of his perfectly formed mouth.

"Megan should suffice."

"Megan, do you know that Arthur has decreed that any magus who is caught will be burned alive at the stake without trial?"

A hiss escaped my lips as my blood began to simmer.

"How is it that you know this?" My eyes narrowed as I awaited his reply.

Merlin studied me, seeming to read the very pages of my soul.

"I divined it, Megan."

If he had been anyone else, I might not have believed him. Not until I'd seen the decree for myself. But there was no doubting Merlin. Arthur had hit a new low. It was one thing to exile the magi, but to order such a brutal and final punishment for something we were born with was deplorable.

My head ached as I tried to reconcile my brother with his actions. I searched and searched for a solution, but none would occur without bloodshed.

"Megan," Merlin started. "I would advise against starting a war with your brother." The great sorcerer must have somehow seen that I'd settled on a violent solution, though it was not what I'd wanted.

Defiance flooded my veins. "You think I *want* to shed blood? Arthur started this war. I intend to finish it." My voice rang with the power of truth and conviction.

"Will you risk the lives of your people?" Merlin asked softly.

I scoffed. "My people are already at risk! How many lives will be stolen if I sit idly by? What would that accomplish? They would die for nothing!" My chest heaved with each breath. "If we don't go on the offensive, Arthur will hunt us all down. That includes you, Merlin. Wouldn't you rather fight for a chance to live than hide away, always looking over your shoulder and wondering if *this* is the day you die? Tell me, *sorcerer*, do *you* have a better plan?"

Merlin hung his head in thought. "How about a compromise?" His head still lowered, he raised heavily lidded eyes to look at me.

I focused my most threatening stare on him, willing him to continue even though I highly doubted he could contrive an acceptable compromise.

He raised his head. "I will provide training for you and the other magi. You're already a gifted sorceress, but I can improve your skill and knowledge tenfold. We will do things your way, but understand that I will not fight."

To my surprise, I found this to be an acceptable arrangement. Hope took root in my dual hearts. We shook on it and headed back to camp with the wood in tow. It was time to take back my throne and all it stood for.

Revealing my identity to my people was a huge relief. When Guinevere made the announcement and I released the glamour, each and every magus went down on one knee. I addressed the crowd.

"Arthur has stolen the throne, but he has not stolen our strength, our pride, or our future." The magi erupted in cheers, but I continued. "Arthur has declared that all captured magi will be burned at the stake."

Angry and fearful silence ensued.

"Don't let this snuff the fire in your souls!" I began to pace, my own soul fire burning and urging my legs to move. "Let this fire burn in your veins! I need warriors, even if you're not yet trained. If you have the spirit of a warrior, I need you. Your kingdom needs you. Your families need you." I drew a line in the pebbly sand. "All who will fight alongside your queen, come! Stand by my side!"

A rush of men, women, and even children came to my side. I was proud to have so many answer the call. I wouldn't allow the children to fight, not the way the adults would, but they would have their place in this war. In fact, the only ones who did not answer were those physically incapable of participating in a war. They would have their place too.

I lifted my arms, requiring silence. "I have one more announcement to make. Or rather, an introduction. I have here with me the most renowned sorcerer in all of Camelot. Fellow Draconians, I give you Merlin."

A silent and reverent awe covered the crowd, but soon whispers of excitement cut through it like a hot knife through butter. Every last magus crowded around Merlin, wanting to shake the hand of the most powerful sorcerer in existence. It was a story they could pass down to their descendants for generations. Merlin was kind to let them have this. I would allow it too, for now. But soon, very soon, we would have to begin training. The longer we waited, the more innocent lives would be lost.

Over the next two moon cycles, Arthur sent some of his men to hunt and capture magi. Between my magic and Merlin's, the glamour over the camp held true. Other refugee camps weren't so lucky. On occasion, Merlin saw in the stars the capture, torture, and subsequent deaths of many magi, as well as any who harbored them.

The magi in my camp worked together nicely, each doing their part. The children who had answered the call were useful and as vital to our mission as any adult, and I never missed a chance to let them know it. Some were old enough to have learned some skills in weapon making. Yes, we had magic, but not every battle could be won that way. Sometimes, we had to fight: hand to hand, weapon against weapon, fire with fire.

"Your Majesty!" Terrance, recently thirteen, rushed over to me. He'd barely begun to develop scales along his jawline. He held up a bow and quiver of arrows.

"Terrance!" His sister, Elena, ran up behind him, out of breath. "Terrance," she whispered loudly, a scolding clearly on its way across her lips. "One does not simply approach Queen Morgana. Where is your etiquette?"

Elena scoured Terrance with a look, though it hardly daunted him. He was clearly struggling to not roll his eyes.

"Forgive me, Your Majesty." Terrance bowed. "If Her Highness is willing, I would be very pleased to show you my latest handiwork."

I couldn't help but smile broadly. "Terrance, I would be delighted."

Terrance threw a smug look in Elena's direction. Before Elena could get too embarrassed, I added, "However, your sister is right. Without etiquette, we have no order. Without order, we have anarchy. What should I have you do as penance?"

Elena beamed as Terrance's expression grew nervous.

"Let me see what you've made, Terrance, and then I'll decide what to do with you," I mused.

He presented the weapon he'd made, and it was beautiful. The bow was made of the finest wood. I drew back the string as though I would fire an arrow, though I didn't have one nocked. The movement felt perfect. I would have been impressed had this finery come from an adult. I was pleasantly flabbergasted that it had been made by a child.

"You made this, Terrance?"

He nodded vigorously. "Yes, Your Majesty. I believe it's my best work yet."

I studied the piece a moment longer. "This is fine work." I brought my thumb and forefinger to my chin in thought. "I'd like to keep this. It will be the price for your lack of propriety."

Terrance smiled and bowed. "It pains me to part with it, Your Majesty. However, I will use this opportunity to learn a lesson in propriety and dishonor you no further."

This kid is a marvel unto himself.

He took my silence as a dismissal and taunted his sister all the way back to the lakeshore.

"Impressive," Merlin said, nearly startling me.

"Isn't it?" I turned my attention to my new weapon.

"Yes, I suppose the bow is impressive as well, but I mean you, Your Majesty."

I lifted my eyes and met his—bright, fiery, and intense, much like the dragons we had descended from. I cleared my throat and looked at the bow again. "What are you on about?" I dared another glance at him and found his gaze had softened.

"You're incredible to observe. The way you interact with your subjects. You've found a balance between being their ruler and being one of them."

"I *am* one of them." I turned my attention to my fellow magi, who milled about, made preparations, and practiced the skills Merlin had taught them. "I'm proud to be. They're good people, eager and willing to do what's right."

"You *are* one of them, yet you are so much more."

A vision of the two of us entwined beneath a private willow flashed into my mind. It wasn't my vision, but I didn't mind. We exchanged a knowing smile. Just as Merlin was about to speak again, Guinevere interrupted, her eyes wide with panic. I'd never seen Guinevere ruffled before.

"Your Majesty, I have news."

"What is it, General?" I asked, dreading the answer.

"Arthur has put out a bounty of three hundred scales for any magus caught and turned over to his guard."

My face blanched. Did Arthur's hatred and cruelty really go so deep?

"There's more, Your Highness." Guinevere stole a glance at Merlin before returning her gaze to me. She seemed to struggle with forcing words from her mouth.

"Out with it, General." I sighed and rubbed my fleshy palm, now sweating, over my face.

"Arthur has discovered you're alive. He's offering six hundred scales for you—dead or alive. An extra four hundred if the bounty hunter delivers your head on a stake."

I lost feeling in my limbs. Arthur and I had rarely gotten along, but this . . . this was incredible.

"Maybe we should go somewhere more private to process this new development," Merlin offered.

I noticed eyes on me. My people were seeing me in distress.

Guinevere nodded in agreement and took off toward my tent. Merlin lightly placed his hand at the small of my back, guiding me while my brain tried to wrap around the idea that Arthur truly wanted me dead. To call the situation difficult was a severe understatement. What would my parents have said if they knew Arthur was trying to kill me?

What would they have said if they realized my only option was to kill him first? I did have to kill him, I realized. He would never give up, and with the level of support he had from nonmagical Draconians, no jail would hold him.

I sat on a simple stool, a temporary replacement for my throne. Guinevere and Merlin sat in silence, allowing me to work through this new development. There really wasn't anything to work through, though. Arthur wanted me dead, and nothing would change his mind. He was always so stubborn. If he killed me, he'd continue hunting the magi and destroy them, one by one.

There were things that needed to be said, but I couldn't bring myself to say them aloud. I couldn't find the words. Eventually, Merlin and Guinevere began speaking to each other in hushed tones. Still trying to find my words, I ignored them.

It seemed like minutes had passed, but when Guinevere pulled the tent flap open, I saw that it was nightfall. I'd been in there for hours. Dazed, I glanced around. Merlin was no longer in the tent.

"Where's Merlin?" I asked.

"He's left, Your Highness," Guinevere replied.

"When?"

"Some time ago."

"Where did he go?"

"I'm not sure, Your Majesty."

"When will he return?"

"I'm not sure of that, either. We had a heated discussion about what to do next. I told him we would fight. He told me you already knew he would not fight alongside us. Is this correct?"

I nodded. Had Merlin abandoned us? Me?

"I felt far less fear when I thought he would fight alongside us." Guinevere frowned, and she looked truly exhausted. "Your Majesty, we need to address this with the people. They deserve to know the dangers, and of Merlin's departure."

I nodded. "Gather them. I'll speak to them."

"I have news that may shake some of you to your core." I studied my army, gauging their reactions.

"Arthur has now decreed a bounty for the delivery of any magus. Double the price for me specifically. More, if they deliver my head on a stake."

Their gasps sent ice through my hearts and quickly into my veins.

"What's more, we no longer have the support of Merlin."

There was real fear in their eyes now. Hope leaked from them like wine from a gaping hole in a wineskin.

"I understand your fears. I implore you to embrace this fear and use it to fuel you for the mission at hand. It has not changed. We will still march on Camelot and take back what's ours. We will live in peace and freedom once more."

I wasn't sure I convinced myself, let alone the crowd.

"I will be sending spies to Camelot to get a feel for the atmosphere there. If you are interested in such a position, please speak with the general."

With that, I retreated to my tent.

Six Days Later

"Your Majesty."

I would not be pulled from sleep.

"Your Majesty, it's urgent."

I threw an arm over my eyes, a growl rumbling in my chest. "What is it, Guinevere?"

"One of the spies has returned."

I sat up. "One?"

Guinevere nodded solemnly.

"The others?" I'd sent a total of five.

"Dead, Your Majesty."

"The survivor?"

Guinevere shook her head. "Terrance didn't make it."

My hearts sank as the fire in my veins boiled my blood.

"Any news of Merlin?" I asked, my voice monotone and shoulders sagging.

"I'm afraid not, my queen."

I nodded. "I will address the people."

The magi did not receive the news well. Fear had already gripped them; now it suffocated them. I was losing against an ordinary Draconian, and we no longer had the power and expertise of the great Merlin.

I personally held myself responsible for the deaths of my spies, especially Terrance. Their blood weighed heavy on my hands, and I would carry the burden of guilt for as long as I lived. Which would not be much longer if Arthur had his way.

What could I do? The one spy that remained had only survived because Arthur wanted him to deliver a message: *Give yourself up, and I will take the magi as my slaves rather than destroy them. If you refuse, you will all burn.*

Neither of those choices were acceptable. I would not give my people up as slaves, nor would I allow them to die at the stake. I was lost and without hope. My only choice was to take Arthur on directly.

"I genuinely advise against this, my queen." Guinevere's voice quaked.

Exhausted, I rubbed my forehead. "There's no other choice, General. I must do this for my people, or we will cease to be."

"There's always another way."

"You sound like Merlin." I stood and began pacing my tent. "If there is another way, I cannot see its design. There's no time to waste. I must protect my people."

"And what of your people's leader?" Guinevere's voice was on the edge of a shout. "Who will lead them and rule in your stead? There is no one your equal." Guinevere shook, her lower lip quivering almost imperceptibly.

"If I die, Guinevere, you will rule in my stead."

Guinevere's eyes went round as a throwing stone. "Your Majesty, I could do no such thing."

"You can, and you must."

"I cannot talk you out of this awful plan, can I?" My friend spoke quietly.

I shook my head. "No, General. You really can't."

Three Days Later

It was decided. I would have a few warriors escort me near the castle. Once we reached a certain point, they would return to camp, making sure nobody followed. I packed nothing and left with only the clothes on my back, the pride of my people, and the training that Merlin had given before his departure.

My hearts ached at the thought of Merlin. I'd learned so much from him before he deserted us. Even in his passive ways, he knew a lost cause when he saw one, and I couldn't blame him for leaving me. Abandoning our people, however, was less forgivable.

My escorts left me near the edge of the forest with the castle in sight. I created a glamour to keep myself safe. I had to make it to the great hall before I revealed my identity. The plan was clear: get as close to Arthur as possible and take him out. It was simple, but it would never be easy. Even with his blatant disdain for the lives of others, it was difficult to imagine cutting him down. I would, though. I had to. Too much was at stake.

My glamour perfectly in place, I took a step forward, only to halt immediately after. I felt eyes on me—more than one pair. I turned, prepared to fend off Arthur's men. What I saw instead was a line of magi, their magical auras shining brightly around them. Among them were Lancelot, Gawain, and Kay. They wore no glamours, and their intentions were clear in their eyes and postures. They'd made it and would not let me do this alone.

This was Merlin's doing; I was sure of it. It dawned on me then that his departure had been to seek magi who weren't part of our camp. Others who were willing to fight. A grim smile on my face, I let my glamour fall. If they would not disguise themselves, neither would I. I made sure to make eye contact with each one. It was likely that many would die that day.

I turned back toward the castle and marched forward, my fellow magi following my lead.

As we marched on the castle, the outer gate opened to us. Only a small number of ordinary Draconian guards were visible in the towers. It was eerie. We had had more guards during Arthur's coup than were visible now. My brother had always been cocky and he had a habit of underestimating me, but this was downright insulting.

We continued our march on the castle through the outer court, across the moat. The main gate lowered for us, and again I felt insulted. They didn't even consider us enough of a threat to force us through the barbican. A familiar fire heated my blood to a low simmer.

Marching through the gate and the courtyard unscathed, we entered the keep and made our way to the great hall.

There, standing on the dais beside Arthur, was Terrance. I'd thought him dead! I scanned his body, searching for injuries, and found none. His eyes, though, told a different story. There were ways to torture a person—a child—that left no physical marks. My blood began to rage, barely contained within my veins. My brother was a monster.

Guards hovered near Arthur and Terrance, while others lined the hall.

"Welcome home, Sister," Arthur said in mock pleasantry.

I snarled at his mockery.

"Now, now. Is that how we were raised to treat family?" he taunted.

A low growl escaped my burning throat. "You're no family of mine. Release the boy, return my throne, and I'll consider letting you live."

Arthur's eyes narrowed. "*Your* throne?" He nodded to one guard, who brought forth a sword sheathed in a beautiful scabbard atop an ornate red velvet pillow. "I have something that proves otherwise."

I startled at the sight. My sword, Excalibur. It called to me in much the same way Terrance's eyes called for me to rescue him from his abuser.

The guard bowed to Arthur as he offered his usurping king *my* sword. Arthur stood and held the scabbard in one hand, releasing Excalibur from its sheath. It sounded like the whisper of an ethereal song. It glowed in his hand, recognizing its current master.

I sneered at my brother. "You know that Excalibur won't serve you well. It bows to you because it must, but it knows you are not its true master." In that moment, I should have thought of the safety of my people; however, all I could focus on was the memory that goading him had always been the best form of entertainment.

His face went red and then immediately purple. Before I could follow his movements, he ran Excalibur straight through Terrance's gut.

"No!" I attempted to form a ball of fire to launch at Arthur, but when I called to my fire, it never left my hands. It died as soon as it surfaced. Did my hands betray me?

Arthur laughed. "You're powerless here, Sister. I have dragonsbane hanging all over the castle." He stared at me, savoring my reaction.

No. No no no no. Turning my gaze upward, I saw the dragonsbane hanging from the high ceilings. I lowered my head and turned slightly, looking at my fellow magi. I'd led them to their slaughter. I wasn't sure how many had learned hand-to-hand combat. As magi, we rarely needed to fight, but when we did, we had our magic.

Kay caught my eye and bowed. "It has been an honor to serve you, my queen." In the next moment, she took out the nearest guard before grabbing a torch from the wall and setting the dragonsbane ablaze. It was brilliant, but it cost her when one of the other guards took her out. Another magus followed suit and set fire to the dragonsbane on the other side of the hall.

It wasn't long before I felt the familiar fire of magic coursing through my veins, aching to be free. I obliged. I whirled around and hit the nearest guard in the face with a blast of fire so powerful, he crumpled, screaming in agony. I took his sword from its sheath and turned back to face my brother.

Arthur's brows gathered into a terrible mass of mountains on his otherwise handsome face. His lips contorted in rage, he charged at me with Excalibur, and I parried with my newly stolen sword.

"Will you not use your filthy magic, Sister?"

"Not this time, *Brother*. You and your guards will see that magic isn't the only deadly thing I wield with power and precision."

Arthur's eyes looked like they might pop from their sockets. I told him as much. He screamed as he attacked, spittle flying from his crazed mouth. It was foolish of him to get so angry. Such blind rage led to mistakes.

He struck and I blocked. Excalibur wasn't helping Arthur in the slightest. In *my* hands, a death blow would have come easily, no matter the opponent. Again, I told my brother as much.

"Surrender, Brother. This does not end well for you." My plea was genuine. We had never gotten along, but he was still the son of my parents. They had loved him.

"I'd rather die!"

I sighed. "So be it."

We continued our violent dance until I found an opening, grabbed his shoulder with one hand, and ran him through with the stolen sword.

I stared into his eyes as I twisted the blade within his now-open belly. It was slow and agonizing for both of us. Removing the sword slowly, I forced myself to keep my eyes open. I would own this choice for the rest of my life.

Arthur fell to his knees, landing so hard I could hear the bones crack upon impact with the stone floor. He fell to the side. Blood poured from his belly, hot and thick; it trickled from his mouth as he cursed me with his dying breath.

I picked up my favored sword. My blood sang, though my hearts mourned the loss of my brother. Of the way things should have been between us. It was done, and I had a responsibility now.

With Excalibur in one hand and the stolen sword in the other, I climbed the dais and bellowed, "It is over! Arthur is dead. Surrender now or forfeit your life."

Arthur's guards were more ridiculous than he had been. Shouts of "Never!" and "Magi will not rule!" rang through the great hall. A new fury and sadness consumed me in that moment. The fire in my blood went beyond the boiling point, and my body began to change.

I grew larger, my body stretching and aching in the most magnificent way as it became less humanoid. I sprouted a tail—an odd yet pleasant sensation. Claws grew from what were now my four feet, sharp and deadly. Finally, a more serpentine tongue slipped over sharpened teeth. Relishing in this new powerful body covered almost completely in scales, I looked down on my enemies, and they cowered in fear.

One very foolish guard yelled, "No matter what shape you take, you will always be a dirty magus!" They were his final words.

I huffed in his direction, and fire spewed from my mouth, consuming him instantly. It was too good for him, really. He deserved a little more time to consider his life choices.

"Would anyone else like a taste of my fire? It's quite spicy." I scanned the room, looking for volunteers. I found none.

"I accept your surrender. Magi, please escort these traitors to a secure location and guard them. Make sure they are fed and well cared for."

The magi smiled triumphantly and marched the former guards from the great hall. Left alone with the remains of Terrance and my brother, I shifted back into humanoid form. I didn't know what I had become, but it had never happened before. More troubling was that I had not been able to prevent Terrance's death. Twice I mourned him. I grieved for Kay and all the others who had lost their lives in this war. I mourned the loss of my brother as well. I mourned for my parents, who would have been devastated to see this day.

After some time, I felt a pair of eyes on me. When I looked up, the most powerful sorcerer in all of Camelot stood across the hall.

Merlin.

"A little too late, sorcerer." My voice was heavy with the burden of loss.

He said nothing but approached and sat down beside me.

"Where have you been?" I asked, tired.

"Searching for other magi who would fight alongside you."

I chortled. "I thought you were a pacifist."

"I am." He smiled sadly. "But I couldn't let you face Arthur alone. So I found others who had no qualms about fighting side by side with their queen."

"It was most unexpected, but I wouldn't have made it without them. And you found Lancelot, Gawain, and Kay. Thank you." I laid my head on Merlin's shoulder. I was so very tired.

Merlin kissed the top of my head. "Someone set dragonsbane on fire."

"Yes."

"Were you affected?"

"The dragonsbane suppressed my powers, but they came back once enough of it had burned away."

"That's not what I mean, Morgana. Did anything unusual happen to you?"

I told him about my shifting shape. His eyes came alive with excitement.

"Our kind, the Draconians, are descended from magical creatures. Dragons. When a magus inhales the smoke from dragonsbane, it gives them the ability to shift back and forth between our inherited dragon form and our evolved humanoid form. I've never done it, but it sounds exciting!" And he *was* excited. Excited enough for the both of us.

I was merely content to have my throne back. I couldn't care less about changing forms, even if it had sealed my victory. His excitement was endearing and a wonderful distraction from my next task. Perhaps, after everything my people and I had been through in recent moon cycles, repairing a broken kingdom would seem like dragon's play.

The Power of the Sword

Allorianna Matsourani

It was Gwendolyn's time to flourish. She welcomed it, determined to see it through. Now that she had retaken the Red Dragon from Edwain, a powerful lord from the south, Gwendolyn could claim her place as the protector of Cheldric Estate in Glennedd.

Edwain had misjudged her, the small dark-haired daughter of Baldwyn Kennard and younger sister of Garreth Kennard. She had reclaimed the Red Dragon, her late brother's sword, as she and her father fought to take back the land Edwain had purloined from them.

When Edwain had turned his back on her to strike at her father with the Red Dragon, Gwendolyn had gouged his hand with her dagger, inflicting a severe wound that left Edwain dazed and slumped in his saddle. As the sword fell from his grip, she quickly retrieved it and delivered a blow that knocked Edwain from his horse. As he lay face down in the dirt, Gwendolyn held the sword high and claimed her victory.

The Red Dragon was solid and heavy in her hand as she rode her horse up to Cheldric castle to announce the triumph over Edwain and his soldiers. The moment, though, was bittersweet. Cheldric Estate would once again be managed by a Kennard, but the price had been heavy.

The battle had cost her father his life.

Gwendolyn called out to the men and women gathered at the castle gate as she brandished the sword. "Behold the sword of Garreth, bearing the Red Dragon crest of the Kennard family! Know me, Gwendolyn, daughter of Baldwyn Kennard, as the new guardian of the sword and protector of this land—our land."

The murder of her brother Garreth and the capture of their home had happened months earlier, when Edwain had waged battle against them. An archer's arrow had punctured Garreth's heart, and Edwain had looted her brother's lifeless body, taking the Red Dragon to use as his own. Gwendolyn still burned with rage when she thought of Edwain casting her and her father off their land, forcing them to take refuge with neighbors.

At the sound of a horse galloping up the hill, Gwendolyn turned and saw Alain Petyr riding toward the castle. He brought his massive chestnut stallion to a halt at the gate, a few feet from where she sat astride her own mount.

"Gwendolyn, I mourn the loss of your father. He was a good man. He would be proud of you for reclaiming the Red Dragon and taking back Cheldric. But I fear this is not the end. Edwain still lives, and he will stop at nothing to punish you and retake Cheldric. That sword might validate you as Cheldric's rightful owner, but you must remain vigilant."

Gwendolyn nodded and tightened her grip on the sword's leather-wrapped hilt. The Red Dragon had been forged years ago for Garreth by Ezekiel the swordsmith, whose craftsmanship was legendary. His blades were thought to wield mystical power. The Red Dragon's steel blade had been quenched in water from the sacred waterfall at Cheldric and droplets of Garreth's blood. The blade had been polished on grinding wheels fitted with stones from the estate's riverbed. Ahmet, the cutler from Arabia, had etched the image of the Red Dragon from the Kennard coat of arms into the sword's gold pommel.

A portion of that image now bore a rust-colored stain. Gwendolyn believed it to be a drop of Garreth's blood, spilled in his fight against Edwain. Family lore claimed that a drop of blood from a sword's slain owner infused the weapon with extraordinary power. She needed the legend to be true; she was counting on strength from the Red Dragon to help her face and conquer Edwain, should he attack them again.

"With the Red Dragon in my possession, Edwain's defeat is certain if he returns," Gwendolyn said fiercely. "I will avenge the spilled blood of my brother and the death of my father."

Although the words she spoke were strong, Gwendolyn did not feel that strength in her heart. Uncertainty clawed at her, making her stomach clench and her knees tremble.

Alain's presence, though, was a comfort. He had always been a trusted advisor and cherished friend. Now, without her father, Gwendolyn knew she would need Alain more than ever. Alain had opened his estate to Gwendolyn and her father when Edwain had taken Cheldric from them. Gwendolyn was certain she could always count on him to ride beside her against Edwain.

Once they had dismounted and passed through the gate, Gwendolyn led Alain to the great room inside the keep. She retrieved a jar of Cheldric's best wine from a secret buttery hidden behind one wall. She poured some for them both.

As they talked, Gwendolyn held the Red Dragon. She stroked its smooth blade and thought of her father and Garreth. The emotional pain she had endured when losing them was renewed, and her throat tightened as her eyes were overcome with tears. Though she tried to blink them back, a single tear fell from her cheek onto the sword's blade.

At that moment, a surge of power flowed from the sword into her fingertips. The energy was electric, with an intensity so forceful that the shock almost knocked the sword from her hand.

Gale reviewed the words she had just written, imagining how the powerful Red Dragon would protect Gwendolyn and Cheldric. She was contemplating Gwendolyn's next move when she heard a familiar voice.

"Well, that sucks."

Rebelle's comment, as always, had the ability to shear away Gale's confidence and shred her self-assurance into fragments of self-doubt. Although Gale tried to ignore the words, she couldn't help but accept them as true. She had no weapon against this enemy—skepticism over her own ability and worth—which was fed by her relentless insecurity and Rebelle's cruel remarks.

"Why do you say that?" Gale replied defensively. "Gwendolyn has reached a milestone. Her appropriation of the Red Dragon marks a major turning point. The sword gives her strength and will help her protect Cheldric against Edwain."

Rebelle chuckled. A dismal sound, low and mirthless, it sucked the warmth from Gale's body and left her shuddering.

"A turning point?" Rebelle scoffed. "Your attempt to portray Gwendolyn as strong is feeble at best. You have no idea what strength is. You've always been weak."

"Please . . . don't."

"What's the matter, Gale? Think you can fight me and win?" Rebelle's voice, spiteful and nasty, reverberated through Gale's head. "You know I'm right. Don't fight me. You won't succeed."

"I have to try." With great effort, Gale refocused on her laptop and continued to type.

It was late in the evening several weeks later when Gwendolyn's servant knocked on her chamber door and announced that Alain wished to speak with her.

When she passed into the great room, Alain turned from the fireplace and greeted her with a quick embrace. "Gwendolyn, I have information about Edwain's plans."

"Tell me."

"He has enlisted the help of Percival in the south, and they are assembling an army. Edwain is using the gold and silver he amassed from plundering landowners in other shires to hire French soldiers. Percival is paying Vikings from the far north to fight as his mercenaries. Their plan is to take everything you have, including your life.

"Gwendolyn, if Edwain conquers Cheldric, he will surely target my estate next, then Deganway and the other estates, until he controls all of Glennedd. It's time to see Mervin of Deganway, to enlist his support. We must leave immediately."

Devastated by the news, Gwendolyn somehow managed to answer with courage. "Let's ride to Deganway at sunrise, then. I'll send a man to Mervin now to let him know we are coming. But for now, please accept a meal and stay the night. You must be tired."

"More than anything, I am worried," Alain replied. "I don't know how we can put together an army to defeat Edwain, even with Mervin's help."

Gwendolyn went into the secret buttery adjacent to the great fireplace. She emerged moments later with a long, slender burlap bundle, which she unwrapped to reveal the Red Dragon, securely stowed in its wool-lined leather scabbard.

"Alain, I may be foolish, but I truly believe that Garreth's sword has a unique power. I felt an outpouring of power surge through me as I touched the sword's blade."

"That may be so," Alain said. "But can you even wield a sword? And even if you can, is it enough to defeat Edwain?"

"I don't know."

"Then we must not look to magic to win our fight. I have gold we can use to pay Swiss soldiers to battle for us. My hope is that Mervin does as well. And I believe we can enlist the help of others in Glennedd to stand against Edwain."

After Alain had left the room, Gwendolyn continued to sit by the fireplace. She forcefully clasped the sword's grip and once again felt the power of the Red Dragon flow into her. Still, her stomach churned as she mulled over Alain's plan to enlist the help of Mervin and the other residents of Glennedd and hire their own mercenaries. Would that be sufficient?

She carefully replaced the Red Dragon in its scabbard and burlap wrapping and returned it to its hiding place. As she closed the panel to the hidden buttery, a cold filled her that chased all the warmth from her body and left her shivering. She knew the icy chill came from deep-seated dread, a warning that their plan wasn't enough. They would need a miracle to emerge victorious from any onslaught waged by Edwain.

She only prayed the Red Dragon could deliver it.

When Gale closed her laptop, it was past midnight, but she couldn't stop thinking about Gwendolyn and the Red Dragon. She imagined how the etching of the Red Dragon felt under Gwendolyn's fingertips. Electrifying. Sizzling with energy.

But what type of miracle could emerge from the sword?

"You think lightning bolts will shoot from the sword and strike down Edwain and his army?"

"Rebelle? You're still awake?"

"Obviously."

Gale sighed. "Nothing as dramatic as that. I was thinking more along the lines of power from the sword being channeled into Gwendolyn and giving her extraordinary strength to defeat her enemies."

"You don't have the writing skill to pull that off."

"Don't say that. I wish you would give me some encouragement rather than always chopping away at my confidence."

"Wouldn't *that* be a miracle," Rebelle quipped. "Too bad the Red Dragon can't strike me down. I know you'd love that."

"It's just that you torment me day and night."

"I just want to keep you from getting your hopes up," Rebelle answered. "You'll only be devastated when you fail."

Gale closed her eyes and tried to fight back tears of frustration. *Will I ever be able to get rid of her?* It was so hard for Gale to feel positive when Rebelle continually made demoralizing comments.

Rebelle was like an infectious disease that needed to be eradicated. Gale desperately wanted her voice out of her life so she no longer had to feel the destructive emotions evoked by Rebelle's malicious words. The miracle she desperately needed—the miracle she prayed for—was the courage and strength to win her fight against Rebelle and banish her forever.

Mervin studied Gwendolyn and Alain as they shared their information on Edwain's plans and asked him to join them in battle. He felt old and tired and did not want to fight their war. Yet he agreed that Edwain would not be satisfied with just Cheldric and would attack other estates in Glennedd. Eventually, Mervin may have to face his own war with Edwain.

But while Gwendolyn appeared courageous and bold, she lacked the training and experience of a seasoned soldier. She also lacked the gold needed to hire experienced fighters since Edwain had looted her estate. Her war chest didn't have nearly enough to defend Cheldric against Edwain.

Still, it was time to mount an aggressive response that would drive Edwain out of Glennedd and render him unwilling to ever come back.

"Edwain must be stopped," Mervin affirmed. "Did your man indicate when they would start their march on Glennedd?"

"Soon," Alain answered. "Within a fortnight."

"Then we must be ready."

Gwendolyn, Alain, and Mervin discussed their defenses. To defeat the army Edwain had assembled, they would need support from all the landowners in Glennedd. When their discussion ended, it was well past midnight. Mervin suggested Gwendolyn and Alain stay as his guests at Deganway for the next few days so they could continue planning.

As she headed to her assigned guest chamber, Gwendolyn considered their discussion. Without her father and brother, would she have the courage and strength to protect Cheldric against Edwain? Cheldric had been home to her family for generations, and she didn't want the Kennard family legacy to end with her defeat at the hands of a thief.

Gwendolyn knew she had to carry the Red Dragon into battle. Reluctant to take a gamble on her prowess with a sword, she resolved to employ Alain as her tutor and start training as soon as they left Deganway. With her own plan now in place, Gwendolyn's anxiety subsided enough for her to drift off to sleep.

"Alain, I want you to teach me to fight with Garreth's sword," Gwendolyn announced the following morning as she entered Deganway's great room for breakfast.

Alain and Mervin both looked up in surprise. "Gwendolyn, we are planning to hire swordsmen to battle Edwain," Alain said.

"But we need the Red Dragon if we are to be victorious," she replied.

"Then I will carry the Red Dragon into battle."

"No," she insisted. "I must do it."

"Gwendolyn, why do you want to carry your brother's sword into battle?" Mervin asked. "You are not trained as a man-at-arms. The undertaking you propose will be difficult. More than likely, it will be deadly. Are you prepared to make such a sacrifice?"

"You cannot dissuade me," Gwendolyn said. "I know in my heart that the Red Dragon will protect me. With Alain's tutelage, I'll be able to handle the Red Dragon so its power and force can effectively overcome Edwain."

"Very well," Mervin responded. "I'll have my blacksmith prepare a suit of armor for you and your horse."

"But Mervin," Alain interjected, "is this wise? How can a sword impart strength unto her? It sounds like a magician's tale, and I cannot accept it."

Gwendolyn's eyes narrowed with anger. "You have no choice but to accept it. If I don't do everything within my power to protect Cheldric and I lose my home, then I will surely lose my soul and my spirit and I may as well be deceased." She took a breath to calm herself and continued speaking with more control.

"If you won't teach me, I'll find someone else. But you are the best swordsman in Glennedd. My success will be more likely if you instruct me."

Alain reluctantly conceded. "As soon as we get back to Cheldric," he said, "we'll start your instruction in swordsmanship."

Gale sat back and reviewed her work. She felt more confident about Gwendolyn's ability to hold her own against Edwain. But soon Rebelle's voice was intruding into her thoughts and interrupting her focus.

"Alain won't be able to help her, you know. Not in two weeks. That's not enough time for an inexperienced little girl to learn sword fighting."

"Gwendolyn is highly motivated," Gale replied brusquely, trying to ignore Rebelle's uninvited critique.

"Maybe so," Rebelle retorted. "But motivation doesn't always equal success. Look at you. A perfect example."

Gale frowned. "Rebelle, what are you doing here? I really don't have time to listen to your comments. All you do is criticize my work. Just leave me alone."

"You know I can't do that. I make you complete. You couldn't survive without me."

Gale closed her eyes and pictured the Red Dragon. She imagined tracing the lines of the engraved pommel with her index finger. She felt the sword's power surge through her finger, into her hand, and up her arm. Energized, Gale rose from her desk chair and walked over to the hallway mirror to face her aggressor. Rebelle stared back at her defiantly.

"Rebelle, I *can* make it without you, and I will. I told you that Gwendolyn is highly motivated. Well, so am I!"

"Whoa, where did that come from?" Rebelle sneered. "I didn't think you were capable of such intensity."

"You'd be surprised what I'm capable of," Gale countered. "Very surprised. Rebelle, you need to leave me alone. Now."

Gale turned away and went back to her desk.

A week later, plans were finalized for Glennedd's defense. While Mervin recruited help from other residents, Alain and Gwendolyn continued to work on her sword fighting. They practiced basic skills, such as properly gripping the Red Dragon, maintaining a ready position, blocking and parrying, and attacking. They both wore armor to simulate the conditions she would face on the battlefield.

"Remember, Gwendolyn, hold the sword in front of you with both hands, elbows close to your side."

She nodded and repositioned her gloved hands as Alain had instructed. He took a moment to shift her right hand to the cross-guard end of the grip and place her left hand underneath it, closer to the pommel.

"If you grip it this way, your hold will be much firmer. It'll be more difficult for your enemy to strike it from your hand." He lowered the visor of his helmet. "Now attack me."

Gwendolyn obliged, lunging at Alain with a fierce stabbing motion. He immediately moved his sword against hers, knocking the Red Dragon aside.

"When your enemy swipes at you with his sword," he said, "lift your blade against his to block the attack, like I just did. You will need a firm grip to effectively do so.

"Now let's try again. This time, I will attack you."

Alain lunged at Gwendolyn, and she knocked his sword aside and out of the way. She then lifted the Red Dragon high above her head with both hands to deliver a blow to his arm. Alain, however, recovered quickly and touched the tip of his blade to the armor over her heart.

"You should avoid lifting your arms and sword over your head. That move will make you vulnerable to attack."

Gwendolyn paused, discouraged and breathless. "Alain, why don't I feel the power of the Red Dragon? I could be holding any sword in my hands."

"We're just beginning your instruction. Be patient. If the Red Dragon does have the power you speak of, it will come. But you must be ready."

Alain again feigned an attack. Gwendolyn took a deep breath, hoping she would feel the power of the Red Dragon. Instinctively, she blocked his attack with her sword, simultaneously pushing him with her foot to throw him off balance. He regained his step and attacked again, thrusting his sword to meet the Red Dragon. Gwendolyn, however, stepped to her right and brought the Red Dragon down on Alain's arm.

"Excellent!" he exclaimed. "You are learning."

Gwendolyn smiled. "It was the Red Dragon. I surrendered my doubts and let it guide me."

"Then its guidance is admirable. However, we will continue to practice."

Gwendolyn nodded and gripped the Red Dragon with both hands to defend herself from Alain's next attack. This time, she was confident the Red Dragon would not let her down.

Gale stopped typing, knowing the doubt that crept through her thoughts could surface again and enable Rebelle to derail her progress. She visualized the Red Dragon cradled in its scabbard and mounted on the wall just above her desk. She pictured herself taking the sword by the hilt, drawing it swiftly from its leather cocoon, and holding it high.

She imagined she could feel the sword's power as she held it—power that surged through her body's neural network and electrified every cell she possessed. Gale would use the strength of the Red Dragon to fend off Rebelle if she sought to undermine Gale's spirit.

"I will succeed," she said aloud, sensing Rebelle close by.

"You think so?" Rebelle's voice was faint, but loud enough for Gale to hear. "You'll fail again, just like you always do."

"I'm not going to listen to you," Gale asserted. "I'm not going to let you overpower me. I'm stronger than you. I have the strength of the Red Dragon. And I will use it against you if I have to."

"That sword isn't real. You're a fool if you think you could use it to quiet me."

"Maybe, but what have I got to lose?" Gale tightened her grip on the Red Dragon. She got up and faced the hallway mirror, where her doubt was reflected as Rebelle's face.

"Nothing," Rebelle countered. "Because you're nothing."

Gale studied Rebelle's face for a few moments. Abruptly, she extended the Red Dragon and drew an ugly, thin red line down Rebelle's cheek with its tip.

"What . . . have you done?" Rebelle shrieked as her face sagged and blood oozed from the cut. "You'll regret this. You need me. You are nothing without me."

"I have no regrets."

Gale turned away and carefully placed the Red Dragon back in its scabbard. She gingerly touched her own cheek, which stung as though it, too, had been sliced by the sword. When she examined her fingertips, they were clean and unbloodied. She listened for Rebelle's voice but heard nothing beyond the quiet hum of her laptop. Glancing back at the wall where the Red Dragon had been displayed, she found it as bare as an artist's unused canvas.

Less than a week had passed since they finalized their defense plans when Alain knocked on Gwendolyn's bedchamber door in the middle of the night.

"Gwendolyn, I've been notified by my scout that Edwain has started his march. I have sent word to Mervin and the other landowners in Glennedd and asked them to come to Cheldric at once."

Gwendolyn's heart pounded relentlessly as she quickly dressed and sent instructions for everyone in Cheldric to prepare for battle. She retrieved the burlap bundle that held the Red Dragon and went to the great room. Her hands trembled as she drew the sword from its scabbard. Could she successfully wield this sword and protect her beloved Cheldric from her enemies?

"Oh, Father, how I miss you and Garreth. I need you both now more than ever." She fingered the engraved image of the Red

Dragon. "I don't know if I can do this without you. I need strength and courage. If the Red Dragon can deliver a miracle, I need it now."

Soon Alain burst into the great room. "Gwendolyn, Edwain and his army are forty furlongs out and will be here before midday. Mervin and the others have arrived, and our men are gathering at the castle gate."

"We must go, then." She forced herself to sound calm despite her pounding heart and doubts over whether she and her allies had the strength to save Cheldric. Gwendolyn quickly donned her armor, secured the Red Dragon in its scabbard, and attached it to her belt. She then headed out to the stables to saddle her horse.

Although the sun had risen, the light was dim. Dark clouds permeated the sky over Cheldric, and a chilling wind blew from the southeast. The men who had gathered just inside the fortress wall spoke in hushed voices. Their expressions were tense. This wasn't merely a battle to halt Edwain's pillaging; these men would be fighting for their homes and way of life. If Edwain wasn't stopped at Cheldric, the rest of Glennedd would be at risk.

Gwendolyn guided her black stallion to the castle gate and joined Alain and Mervin, who both sat astride strong, swift warhorses. The two were talking quietly, and Gwendolyn silently listened to their plans.

"My man says Edwain has many infantrymen and archers, but his cavalry is small," Mervin was saying. "Most of his army is on foot. He appears to be planning a siege on Cheldric castle as the army is traveling with a battering ram."

Alain nodded. "Then I propose we dispatch our cavalry to wait, out of sight, in back of the stand of trees just beyond the castle's outer wall. While our archers attack the infantry from the parapets, our cavalry can ride in behind Edwain's foot soldiers and disable those charged with deploying the battering ram. If you and I can get to Edwain quickly and incapacitate him, his army will lose its leadership, which may encourage his mercenaries to disband."

Gwendolyn was certain that if she used the Red Dragon to bring down Edwain, the siege would end quickly. As Mervin and Alain continued their discussion, she quietly rode off to position herself behind the trees. When the cavalrymen arrived, she would conceal herself among them and wait for her opportunity to strike Edwain down.

The sky grew darker and the wind increased. Gwendolyn welcomed the faint rumble of thunder and distant flash of lightning, knowing a storm would be advantageous. Rain would obscure Edwain's observation of the landscape, and the curtain of water would help cloak the Glennedd cavalrymen from his view.

As the tempest pressed upon them, the cavalrymen took their positions. Rain started to fall in cold, biting torrents. The cavalry horses, though well trained, became jittery as the thunder grew louder. Their riders, also uneasy, fingered the grips of their swords. Gwendolyn nervously touched her own sword, hoping to slow her racing heart by tracing the lines of the Red Dragon engraved on the pommel. She prayed the Red Dragon would deliver a miracle.

At a shout from one of the cavalrymen, she looked up and saw Edwain's banner just above the crest of the hill. Soon the points of the pikes carried by infantrymen were visible. She glanced at Cheldric's front gate and saw the Glennedd archers taking their positions on the castle's adjacent parapets.

Alain had moved to the front of the cavalry line and was speaking to one of Mervin's men-at-arms. Gwendolyn moved behind the horseman in front of her so Alain would not see her. She was determined that no one, especially not Alain, would keep her from reaching Edwain and cutting him down with the Red Dragon.

As Edwain's infantrymen approached, Alain directed his cavalrymen to move closer to the thicket's edge. The deluge of rain kept them indistinguishable from the trees, and the loud roar of the thunder masked the sounds of the horses. As Edwain's men moved northward toward Cheldric, Alain moved his cavalrymen farther south within the thicket. Soon, the two factions passed each other, and Edwain seemed unaware of Alain's men stealthily moving into position behind his infantry.

From her location near the back of Alain's cavalry, Gwendolyn saw Edwain pass by with several of his knights. They were mounted on black war stallions and rode just behind the line of pikemen. She gradually fell behind Alain's cavalry, then turned her horse and headed north toward Edwain and his knights.

Edwain was in her sight. Undeterred by the stinging rain, Gwendolyn rode forward, pushing her own black stallion into a gallop. She held her reins with one hand and pulled the Red Dragon from its scabbard with the other, careful to keep it low and close to her side. She closed her eyes for a moment.

"Be with me, Father. Pray for me as I advance."

Gwendolyn rode up to Edwain's side. She felt the familiar surge of power flow up her arm from the sword, and with supernatural strength, she raised the Red Dragon against Edwain. He turned to face her, and their eyes locked as she brought the sword down upon him.

"This is to avenge my father and brother!" she shouted. "You will never get Cheldric, as long as I live."

At that moment, Gwendolyn heard a sharp clap of thunder, accompanied by a blinding light. A bolt of lightning snaked down from the darkened sky and struck the Red Dragon's blade at the exact moment it struck Edwain. The force of the thunderbolt knocked the sword from Gwendolyn's grip.

She watched in amazement as the lightning's energy held the Red Dragon aloft, illuminating it in midair as though it were a torch held by an invisible hand. An electrical spark traveled from the Red Dragon's blade into Edwain's armor like a mystical serpent, hissing and glowing as it slithered along.

For several moments, Edwain's entire body blazed a brilliant white, like an otherworldly beacon. Then the light faded, leaving behind a flurry of ashes where Edwain had been. As the white ash dissipated in the wind, the Red Dragon dropped to the ground, unscathed.

"It's Thor!" shouted one of the Vikings. "This invasion has angered him. He will strike us all down. Run!"

Gwendolyn sat motionless, stunned and unbelieving. The

mercenaries turned to flee and were met by Alain's cavalrymen. Sword met sword as the attackers retreated. Blood was spilled and lives were lost, but several of the hired soldiers made their way back down the hill and out of sight. Gwendolyn looked out over the fallout from the battle and saw Edwain's banner on the ground, trampled and forgotten.

As Alain approached her, Gwendolyn felt shaky. Determined to stay mounted, she touched the Red Dragon, which she had managed to safely stow back in its scabbard, and felt its power give her strength.

"What happened?" Alain asked when he reached her side. "I saw Edwain shining as bright as fire, and then he was gone."

"The Red Dragon delivered a miracle. We are safe."

Gale closed her laptop. The Red Dragon had dispatched Gwendolyn's miracle and had done the same for Gale. Rebelle was gone. Gale welcomed her newfound assurance, determined to see it through. This was her time to flourish.

Gift of Language

Dorothy Tinker

There was a time when dragons roamed our lands, speaking the world into form through their creative wisdom.

These days, only my family remembers the dragons and the wisdom they passed to mortal men. We remember the gifts that shaped the world and the way the Darkness formed in the wake of those gifts.

Some believe the gifts created the Darkness. I—

"Lunga! Stop messing around back there and come help me with dinner!"

I grimace as my quill jerks across the parchment, tearing a rip through the middle of it. Sighing, I set the quill in the holder beside my inkwell. The urge to yell right back swells within my chest, but I beat it down. Arguing would only get me extra chores and my quills, ink, and parchment locked away. At least if I go help with dinner, I can write before bed.

"Coming!" I shout before Mother can call me again. Quickly tidying up my desk—hiding away the day's attempts at storytelling—I hurry from my room and down the hall toward the kitchen.

"There you are!" Mother's gaze is as sharp as her words when I enter the kitchen. "You'll never get a proper husband if you stay hidden in your room with those parchments all day."

I withhold a retort as I take up the risen dough waiting for me on the counter. It's the same argument Mother trots out every day. It never matters to her that I'm only eighteen and marriage is the last thing on my mind.

None of the others are married yet, and she coos all over them.

Of course, the "others" are my six (much) older brothers—Wesley, Philip, Hugo, Reece, Heath, and Cole—so that's not surprising. An independent man, especially one as well off as they are, is not so strange.

But an independent woman? Whoever heard of such a thing?

I roll my eyes, careful to keep my back to Mother so she doesn't see. Even that is likely to earn me separation from my writing materials.

"Your father is due back this evening," Mother suddenly says. "I want the house presentable when he arrives."

I spin around, my fingers spasming around the soft dough in my hands. "Really?" Excitement beats beneath my breastbone.

"He sent word two days ago." She huffs and motions me back to the counter. "I'm sure he'll be eager to share any . . . stories with you when he returns."

I don't miss the grimace that crosses Mother's face as she speaks of stories. She's never been comfortable with my gift.

Sometimes I wonder what would have happened if Father had listened to Mother's pleas when I was a babe and not taken me—first daughter born to the Dragonspeak family in generations—before the Slumbering Dragon to accept the seventh dragon gift. Would I still have loved stories and language as much as I do? Would Mother have cared, either way?

Then again, what if I'd been born a son? Would the gift of Language still be scorned in my hands?

A loud snap and flicker of motion before my eyes jerk me from my spiraling thoughts. Mother glares as she drops her hand from between us. "Stop daydreaming, Lunga. We have dinner to make and a house to clean."

I duck my head and turn back to the counter. My mind, however, continues to range. Distracted now from thoughts of my gift, I consider what stories Father might share with me. Clashes with the darkness? Court drama? Darkness among the court?

The images dance and multiply within my mind like fire, eating away the hours as I help Mother make dinner and clean our sprawling cottage. Even ten years after my youngest brother moved away, there are still plenty of beds to make, floors to sweep, and surfaces to dust. And plenty of tedium. It's only the liveliness of my imagination that keeps me from giving in to boredom and curling up in an unused room to sleep and maybe pass on into the next life.

At least the next one might be interesting.

I'm just finishing up in my youngest brother's old hoard room—the room at the very back of the cottage, where I still manage to find the occasional collection of metal, herbs, or coin after all these years—when a *creak* and *thump* sound from the front of the house.

"Melinda! Lunga!"

"Father!"

I drop my dust rag and race toward the front of the house. My father, a large man with fiery red hair and a wide smile, awaits me there with open arms. He's a warm and welcome sight, and I throw my arms around his neck.

He laughs, wrapping himself around me. "Lunga. How is my little dragon tongue?"

I pull back and grin up at him. "Eager to hear of your adventures, Father."

He tilts his head back and gives a hearty guffaw. "Are you now? And what makes you so sure they'll be good enough for your ears?"

My grin eases into a smile. "Because your stories are always exciting. Plus, you're wise enough to know what I'm looking for."

Father sighs, sobering. "Yes, I do know." He gives me a piercing look. "A way out of here and into your own gift."

Heat suffuses my face, and I turn away. "Father . . ."

He pats my back. "There's nothing wrong with your need for independence, dragon tongue. One day, you'll even find it. But for now—"

"For now," I interrupt, "I'm stuck cooking and cleaning a house that's too large for the number of people living in it."

I plant my hands on my hips. "I'm stifled here. I'm not meant for a home and a husband. I'm meant to be out there, like you and my brothers, helping the kingdom fight back the darkness. Language wants to be used. It seeks its purpose. It . . ."

The words die in my throat as heavy sadness settles on Father's face. Only then do I realize what words spill from my lips, flowing through me as though Language has a mind of its own.

But it does, doesn't it? It teaches me and empowers me, and it knows what needs to be done. Why . . . why does that have to be a bad thing?

Father steps closer and frames my face in his hands. I struggle to hold his gaze. "Dragon tongue—Lunga. This is why you're still here. I know," he adds forcefully, as though I would interrupt him, but my throat feels too full. "I know you are chafing, but until you can fully master your gift and integrate it—until it is no longer independent of you—you won't be able to fight the darkness alone."

Pressure tightens around my eyes, but I hold back the tears that threaten. My thoughts dart back to the spiral that plagued me earlier when I spoke with Mother. It has never been just that I was born a daughter of the Dragonspeak family, or just that the Slumbering Dragon gave me this particular gift.

That I was born female and bear the dragon gift many consider evil—that is what my mother, among others, fears and disdains.

"Give it time," Father says, pulling me from my darkening thoughts. "Remember how long it took Cole to master his gift? How long it took for him to understand the good the gift of Hoarding could do?"

I nod. For years growing up, my youngest brother was accused of thievery, lying, and kleptomania. He never actually stole anything or even really lied—except maybe by omission—but by the time I was old enough to remember, he had claimed the deepest room in the house for his collections. The space was more items than air, and no one but he had known what all existed within it.

It wasn't until ten years ago, when he was twenty, that the collections finally showed their true usefulness. A plague had ravaged a nearby village, a plague that even my second youngest brother, Heath—the sibling blessed with the fifth dragon gift, Life—couldn't tame on his own. Cole had delved into his hoard room and, minutes later, produced a collection of rare and quality herbs that were just what Heath needed to beat back the plague and save the village.

After that, Cole worked with the rest of our brothers, putting together hoards for each that would aid them in their work. After learning the value of Cole's hoards, other villages began calling on him, asking him for direction on hoarding food for winter, money for goals, or anything else they could think of. He became known for his need to preserve and eye for quality, and now even the king calls on Cole to help preserve our kingdom's most precious artifacts.

I sigh, my shoulders hunching. "Patience," I mutter. "Patience and work." I shake my head and peer up at Father. "Those I could handle, you know. It's Mother's insistence that—"

I blink as Father jerks his head around. "What is it?"

"Your mother," he whispers. "I called her name when I first got home. Usually . . ."

I cast my own gaze around, but there's no sign of her from where we stand. "Mother?" I call, pulling back from Father's embrace. "Where—"

I bite my tongue. In my movement, I've caught sight of some parchment sitting on the kitchen counter. It wasn't there earlier. Even if it had been, my mother would have thrown it away. It's what she used to do to discourage my stories; I've long since learned to keep my writing materials out of her domain.

Without saying a word, I step into the kitchen and gingerly pick up the folded parchment. As I open it, my breath catches in my throat.

"Lunga?"

I lift my eyes to my father, and he rushes to my side, curling an arm around me in comfort. "What is it?"

I don't answer—I can't. Instead, I flatten the note so he can recognize the symbols that sprawl across the page. Symbols of a tongue abandoned long ago and now spoken only by the Darkness.

And me.

"But how could this even happen? How could darkness sweep into our home, snatch Mother, and leave without a trace?"

I hunch my shoulders against Hugo's lashing demands. My third oldest brother—the older of a pair of twins—has always had a temper to match the heat of his gift, and I've never enjoyed its release.

"Calm down, Hugo," Wesley commands. My oldest brother, who was gifted with Wisdom like every firstborn Dragonspeak before him, shakes his head. "We all know darkness can reach anywhere; that's why we must be strong in the face of it."

"But our family home?" asks Reece. His voice is as soft and chilly as his twin's was loud and fiery. "We're the Dragonspeaks. If darkness doesn't fear us—"

"Enough."

I lift my eyes to Father, who stands in the doorway between the family room and the entrance. Behind him, looking ruffled, are Philip and Cole. Cole doesn't look happy, but I'm not surprised since our second oldest brother had to fly him back from his latest hoarding venture.

"Arguing will get us nowhere," Father says, gesturing Philip and Cole into the family room. Cole sits on the settee beside me, clutching his bag tightly in his lap, while Philip merely leans against a wall. "Your mother is missing, and the Darkness has admitted to taking her."

"But which darkness?" Heath asks. "There are so many; which has claimed to have taken Mother?"

"*The* Darkness," I answer. I open the parchment I found on the kitchen counter and study the runes within for perhaps the fiftieth time tonight. "It's not just an agent of darkness or someone infected with it. It's the original perpetrator."

Wesley shakes his head. "Lunga, that's impossible. The original perpetrator was human, just like us."

I glance at Father, who meets my gaze and sighs. Unlike most of my brothers, he's read ancient texts.

"What?" demand a few voices from around the room.

"He may have once been human," Father whispers, "but the original perpetrator used the dragon gifts to make himself immortal."

"It's why the dragons left," I add, thinking back to the story I was writing when Mother called for me. My heart aches just remembering her voice. "They saw what their teachings had wrought and decided this land was better off without them."

"But why would the Darkness take Mother?" Wesley asks. "Surely it—he—knows such an act would bring the wrath of the Dragonspeak family down upon him."

"No."

We all turn to stare at Father then, even me. "What do you mean, no?" I ask before anyone else can.

"I mean, our family will not be seeking him out."

"What?" The demand spills from seven throats. Father only shakes his head.

"The Darkness knows who we are, or he would not have come for us. I will not risk an entire generation of Dragonspeak on rescuing your mother from the Darkness."

"But, Father," I hiss. "The letter. If we don't go after him within two days, he'll kill Mother. You had me read that to you seven times."

He turns to me with a wan smile. "Yes, dragon tongue, I know. I also remember the rest of what he wrote. 'Only one who bears all dragon gifts can defeat me, so let us see you try.' Which is why I'll take pieces from each of your hoards when I go myself to fetch your mother."

Protests rise throughout the room, but Father lifts his arms and shakes his head to quiet us all.

"My children. My dragonborn. I will not risk losing you and leaving this land vulnerable to the Darkness, do you hear me?" We answer with sullen silence. "Am I understood?"

Soft sighs flit among us, and Wesley whispers, "Yes, Father."

"Good. Now, I want each of you to fetch me the most powerful pieces from your hoards. The more quickly we gather what I need, the sooner I can leave to face the Darkness and retrieve your mother."

We all murmur in quiet agreement, and my brothers turn to the packs they carry with them everywhere. Each of them has spent years using his gift to fight back the darkness, so they no doubt know what pieces would help Father most.

I, on the other hand . . .

"Oh, and Heath," Father adds as I turn listlessly toward the bedrooms, my mind dancing over what little I can claim as a hoard. "Do you have any of those energy potions you make? I spent the day traveling . . ."

I lose track of the conversation as I push past my bedroom door. For a long moment, I just stand there, staring sightlessly at the desk on the far side. Only hours ago, Mother was shouting at me to leave my writing and come help with chores. Now she's gone—taken while I was daydreaming—and Father's about to follow, alone and barely armed . . .

I should at least be going with him. There's nothing I could give him that would count as my gift—at least, not that he could use.

Embroiled in such thoughts, I wander over to my desk and duck underneath it. Pulling up a loose floorboard, I stretch my fingers inside. They shift past parchment, quills, and a couple of heavy inkwells before finally closing on something thick and supple. Smiling grimly, I pull out one book and then another, both made of sturdy leather wrapped around cream parchment.

Sliding out from under my desk, I take a moment to study them. The cover of the first reads *History of the Darkness*. The other cover is blank, but a quick flip to the front page reveals neat handwriting spelling out *The Dragon Speaks*. Both books are old, given to me by Father, and I wonder if I should just give them back to him, though I can't imagine he'd have time to reread them now.

A quiet knock sounds at my door before I can decide. Glancing over my shoulder, I grimace when I see Philip standing in the doorway.

"Is Father getting impatient to leave?"

Philip smirks. "Actually, Heath gave Father a sleeping potion. You should get ready; we're going after Mother ourselves."

With that, he disappears from the doorway.

"Wait! What?" I scramble up from the floor, but before I can reach the hallway, Cole appears.

"I've already checked everyone else's hoards. Want help with yours?"

I flush and wave a hand toward my desk, where the loose plank is still unseated. "Help yourself, I guess, though I don't know what hoard you could possibly compile for me that would help us rescue Mother."

Cole flashes me a boyish smile. Then he produces a knapsack from a pocket that shouldn't have been able to hold it and dives under my desk.

Five minutes later, he's pushing the sack into my hands and propelling me out the bedroom door. He doesn't stop until we're in the family room, where he hurries off to find me some "proper rations."

Curious, I open the sack and peer inside. Parchment, quills, and inkwells are neatly bundled on one side, but it's the two books I was debating giving to Father that catch my eye.

"The writing materials are just basics for you," Cole says as he returns with some dried food, a sheathed knife, and flint and tinder. He lowers them into my sack and pulls out the two books. "These, though . . ." He shakes his head. "I'm not sure what they are, but they were practically screaming that they'd be needed."

He presses them into my hands as Wesley, ever the planner, asks him to verify that we have everything we might need. As Cole bounds off for a final hoard check, I stare at the books.

How could two books make that big a difference?

Finding the Darkness turns out to be our first obstacle. As easily as it is for me to decipher the directions the Darkness provided—"the darkest dell within the deepest forest"—it takes Wesley's Wisdom and Philip's Flight to figure out where exactly that might be.

As we travel, I walk alongside the twins, who illuminate our path: Hugo providing light with his flames and Reece magnifying it with his ice crystals. The magnified light is enough for us to see where we're going—and for me to read the cramped script in the two ancient books. If Cole thinks they're important for the battle, I'm determined to figure out how.

By the time we reach the dell, though, I'm no closer to finding an answer. And Hugo and Reece struggle to light even a body length of earth around us.

"Be careful," Wesley insists as we pause upon the dell's upper lip. "Remember, Mother's safety is our first priority, then our own. If we can defeat the Darkness, we will, but he's plagued our land for millennia. Another day of his presence is not unacceptable."

We all nod silently. My brothers heft the weapons that best complement their gifts—swords, bow and arrow, throwing knives, staff—and I reluctantly clutch the knife Cole gave me before we left. Once Wesley is certain we're prepared, he motions us forward, and we creep down the wooded bank into the shallow depression that the Darkness has claimed for his own.

It feels like we're drawn into the darkness of the dell, to what Cole insists is a large clearing, though it's no less dark for its openness. As we reach the tree line, Wesley motions for us to stop and then for Hugo to extinguish his fire, which seems to hardly encircle us with light now.

Fully engulfed in darkness, I struggle to make out the forms of my brothers as they fan out in front of me along the tree line.

Whispers pass between them, Wesley offering strategy, Philip planning to fly, the twins discussing ways to mingle their Fire and Ice.

They all quiet, though, when Heath speaks of Mother.

"I can feel her," he hisses. "Out in the center of the clearing. She's scraped up, but otherwise fine."

"Can you sense anything else?" Wesley asks.

Silence answers him for long enough that I squirm, pressed up against a thick trunk.

"I . . . think so? I mean, there's definitely something near her, but it's not exactly Life. More like—"

Fire blooms within the clearing. The light from it silhouettes my brothers' forms, and one of them screams.

Curses break from my brothers' lips. Against the light of now-billowing flames, I see Philip leap into the air and disappear into the darkness above. The rest of my brothers scatter, though Heath, whose staff drags behind him, moves slowly, and I realize the earlier bloom of fire was an attack.

I plunge my teeth into my bottom lip and press myself more tightly against the ancient trunk. Each of my brothers has spent years fighting back the darkness. This is a fight they've spent their lives training for. Yet as I watch them throw themselves against a darkness I can't even see, I quake.

We're not ready. How could we think we were ready?

Fire and ice flash, sometimes brightly, sometimes faintly. Without a doubt, I know the fainter attacks belong to the twins, while the brighter ones surely come from the Darkness. I hear the faint twang of a bowstring high above and the soft, distinct *thumps* of arrows and throwing knives making contact with earth and wood—not flesh. I see the occasional dart of a body silhouetted against the blaze in the center of the clearing, but I can't recognize who it is before it disappears again.

Suddenly, a scream cuts through the air, sharper than the one that began the battle. A heavy thud follows, then the sharp rustle of something plowing through dead underbrush. A second scream comes not long after, and then a blazing torrent of dancing fire and glittering ice joins the central blaze in lighting up the clearing.

What it reveals makes me shudder.

Philip lies face-down on one side of the clearing, his limbs sprawled awkwardly. Heath crouches closer to me, one arm slung around his staff as he cradles the other, from which a ragged bone protrudes.

In the middle of the fire-ice vortex, Hugo and Reece stand back to back, their swords lost as they try to fight back the elements surrounding them with raised arms. The sounds of pain ripping from them warn me that their gifts are failing them.

That still leaves two of my brothers, though, and I turn my head in search of them. A yelp catches my ears before I spot either of them. Suddenly, Cole is hanging upside down in midair as though an invisible giant had hold of his ankle. He's flung back and forth through the air, and a stream of objects pours from his pockets.

By the time the stream dissipates and Cole falls still in the air, a steady groan is rolling off his lips.

That's when I finally spy Wesley, almost on the opposite side of the original blaze. He's crouched beside something I can't see from where I stand, and I step away from the tree trunk to strain for a better look.

The moment I realize Mother is kneeling in the grass beside him, Wesley goes flying.

The Darkness found him.

As Wesley's body crunches against a tree trunk, laughter echoes through the clearing. It's dark and deep, and cold races through my chest in its wake.

"This is the fabled Dragonspeak clan?" The words are cold and dark, and the world seems to dim, though fire still blazes within the clearing. "When I heard all seven dragon gifts had been disbursed, I didn't think you would make your destruction so . . . easy."

None of my brothers answer, and I'm frozen where I stand. The dark voice clucks sharply, and abruptly a dim light permeates the clearing.

I flinch and blink against the sudden light. As I adjust to it, I realize ice crystals permeate the air of the clearing, dispersing the light of the fires more evenly.

In the middle of the clearing, not far from the original blaze, stands a man with ebon hair, pale flesh, and eyes that flash like blood in moonlight. I've never seen his image or read his description, but as soon as I see him, I know him.

The Darkness. The original perpetrator.

Blood-red eyes scan the clearing, pausing on each of my brothers. After turning in a full circle, he settles his gaze on Heath, whose fingers press on a wound that no longer shows bone.

"I only count six of you." The words drip like sludge from the Darkness's pale lips. "Don't tell me you were fool enough to leave behind the Language-bearer, useless as the gift may be."

I can't see Heath's face, but he bows his head and leans heavily against his staff. If the Darkness finds an answer in his silence, I can't divine it.

The Darkness sneers and turns to Mother, who still kneels near the blazing fire. In the dim light, I can see her shaking.

"Are these the children you spoke so proudly of, Melinda Dragonspeak?" he taunts. "Boys who bring sharp toys and weak gifts to fight me?" A low, dark chuckle fills the clearing. "Perhaps I should reward you for helping me end the Dragonspeak line with a quick death before I fully dispatch of your children."

He raises a hand and curls the fingers in toward the palm. Between them sprouts a ball of flame that glitters as though it's been enhanced with ice. As I watch, the color of the flame turns from red to blue, creeping toward white, and the glitter sharpens. With each shift in the color and glitter, my chest tightens, until I can barely breathe.

If that fireball touches Mother, she'll die.

The Darkness grins down at Mother, and something within me snaps. Heat flushes through my chest, and my thoughts turn swift, dancing like crystals through my mind. As the Darkness pulls back his arm to throw the fireball, I step toward the clearing.

"Stop!"

The word reverberates from my lips, and the Darkness stills. I myself nearly stop as surprise rings through my crystalline thoughts. That wasn't my native tongue but the forgotten one.

Despite my surprise, I keep walking. As I approach the Darkness, blood-red eyes slowly turn toward me. They narrow as I come closer, but I don't stop until I'm closer to him than any of my brothers.

"Lunga," Heath whispers, but I ignore the breathy plea. My brothers tried; now it's time for Language to claim its purpose.

Even if I'm still not sure what that is.

"You are the seventh Dragonspeak child, then?" The Darkness's words come slowly, tar sliding across the clearing and threatening to suffocate me. "You are the Language-bearer, who bears the seventh dragon gift?"

"Leave . . . her alone . . ."

Surprised, I glance at Cole, who is still suspended upside down. I was sure he'd be unconscious from the blood rushing to his head.

"Yeah," mutters another voice, and I turn wide eyes toward the fire-ice vortex. Hugo and Reece are barely visible through the churning elements, but they kneel together within its base and glare at the Darkness. "Leave our dragon tongue alone."

The warmth in my chest flushes up my cheeks. Father's usually the only one who calls me that. To hear it from my brothers . . .

A memory of cramped script on cream paper, read by the light of the twins' Fire and Ice, flashes through my mind.

"The gift of Language was once the first of the dragon gifts; now it is the last. Not for reasons of good or evil, but that it alone holds the key to understanding them all."

I gasp as the words click in a way they never have before. *Could that be—*

A dark chuckle cuts across my thoughts. "Dragon tongue, is it? How pretentious, to think a girl such as yourself could rank among dragons."

I barely hear the insult, or the increasing protests from my conscious brothers. My mind is racing through memories of cramped script, piecing them together in ways I never thought to before.

"The dragons themselves spoke the world into form . . ."

"The Darkness took the gifts from dragon tongues and shaped them to his will."

"Only one who bears all dragon gifts can overcome the Darkness."

"That's it."

Silence echoes around me, and I blink as I realize I spoke the words aloud. The Darkness and my conscious brothers alike all stare at me, but I no longer feel the fear I did before.

"What's it?"

The question comes from Heath. I'd flash him a grin, but the Darkness's blood-red eyes watch me narrowly, and I dare not look away.

"The one who bears all dragon gifts. I know what it means."

Red eyes flash wide, and the Darkness lifts the hand still cradling a ball of fire and ice. He's moving slowly, though—an effect, I realize, of my earlier command—and I narrow my eyes to focus on his weapon.

"May fire melt a core of ice and ice extinguish flame."

The Darkness yelps as the white of the flames and the glitter of the ice collide and flash, leaving nothing but a billow of steam and smoke to waft from his palm.

I don't pause to admire the effects of the forgotten tongue, no matter how much I want to. Instead, I turn my focus on the Darkness and speak words—a nursery rhyme, almost—that are half memory and half knowledge gifted by Language.

"Where darkness dwells, may light unveil
an evil sunk deep within . . ."

An earthshaking groan fills the air, and the trees around us shift. Shafts of sunlight begin to pierce the high canopy.

"No!"

The Darkness snarls and flies at me, but he hasn't been paying attention to my brothers. He halts in midair, still a body length away from me, and I can see Philip off to one side, one arm outstretched.

"Hurry, dragon tongue!" Philip gasps out, but I'm already speaking the next line.

"An ancient soul, whose life unfolds
with the purging of its sin."

Held hanging by Philip's gift of Flight, the Darkness can't avoid the growing shafts of sunlight. Where light touches moon-white skin, blisters form, red and bubbling. Red eyes slam shut as tears of blood leak from them. I shudder, but Language isn't finished.

"May good restore, to those before
a secret for dragon life . . ."

"Please."

I falter as the Darkness opens his eyes once more to stare at me with milky-white pupils and irises. His hair, previously ebon, has turned white, and clumps of it drift from his scalp.

"Lunga?"

That's Heath, and I grit my teeth as the plea for Life in Heath's voice wars with the purpose Language seeks.

"Heath, don't," Hugo insists before I can find words in our native tongue to argue. "Let our dragon tongue work."

Heath doesn't answer, and I sigh, releasing the final words.

"That brings us care, a life that's fair,
and removal of this strife."

A voiceless wail distends the Darkness's jaw as the final words beat past my lips. Then his body collapses, millennia of decay disintegrating it before our eyes.

As the remains scatter across the ground, silence echoes heavily in my ears.

Until warm arms embrace me, and my mother's voice cries words of love, apology, and gratitude into my ears.

Once Heath has made sure everyone is in a condition to travel, the trip home is mostly silent, only words of nonsense and comfort passing between us. The questions don't come until all eight of us—siblings and mother alike—are safely home.

It's Father who asks the first one, though he thankfully waits until he has hugged each of us firmly and cried into Mother's hair.

"What were you all thinking? You could have been killed."

I duck my head as my brothers all trade glances. Soon, I can feel their eyes on me.

"We nearly were," Wesley finally says. "We would have been if not for our dragon tongue."

Father's mouth hangs open for only a moment before he firms his jaw and turns to me. I lift my gaze to meet his, and he searches my eyes.

"You mastered your gift?"

Out of the corners of my eyes, I see my brothers start to nod, and I bite my lip. When I shake my head, they all start.

"Then how—"

"I don't think Language can be mastered, Father." I think of the knowledge Language provided when I needed it most and smile. "Language isn't a gift you can fully integrate. It's a gift to listen to and learn from."

Father nods slowly and smiles. "Then tell me, how did you use your gift to save everyone?"

"She didn't just save us," Philip interjected. "Father, Lunga defeated the Darkness herself."

I open my mouth to argue that Philip helped, but he casts me a quelling glance.

"Yes, and I'm still not quite sure how."

I turn to Mother, who watches me with warmth and tears in her eyes. Gone is the fear and doubt with which she once regarded me and my gift.

"Will you tell us, dragon tongue?" she asks. "What 'the one who bears all dragon gifts' means?"

My chest feels full as the question sinks in. I smile, even as I blink back inconvenient tears.

"It was all in the ancient texts, really." I motion toward Father. "The ones you gave me for my tenth birthday?"

He nods.

"Well, there are lines I've read time and again since then, but it wasn't until the Darkness was going to kill Mother that I realized what they meant. And then I realized I've never actually spoken the forgotten tongue aloud."

"Because it's the tongue of the Darkness," Father agrees, but I shake my head.

"It's only his tongue because there are no longer dragons to speak it."

Father goes still. "The forgotten tongue . . . ?"

"Is the dragon tongue."

Father shakes his head slowly, more in wonder than denial. "The dragons spoke the world into form . . . with Language." He peers at me. "What can you do with it?"

"You mean, besides destroying the Darkness?" Hugo snarks.

Father frowns at him, but I smile. I spent the trek home thinking about this very question.

"With Language, I Hoard words, which provide great knowledge and Wisdom. With Language, I bring my imagination to Life, freeze the attention of the world upon me, light within it a Fire of understanding and desire, and spur hearts and minds into Flight."

There was a time when dragons roamed our lands, speaking the world into form through their creative wisdom.

These days, only my family remembers the dragons and the wisdom they passed to mortal men. We remember the gifts that shaped the world and the way the Darkness formed in the wake of those gifts.

Some believe the gifts created the Darkness. I believe the Darkness simply grasped them and refused to learn anything else.

Mark of the Hunter

D. Gabrielle Jensen

"Hey!" Fia barked. "Hands to yourself. She's not on the menu."

The construction worker met Fia's gaze and dug his filthy fingers—black beneath the nails and along the cracks of his knuckles—deeper into the other waitress's butt. "Who are you, her mommy?"

She slapped at the meat hook assaulting her coworker, knocking it free. "Yes, and I'll eat you alive if you try it again. She's sixteen."

The man twisted his face, visibly contemplating the new information. The other two men at the table grunted and sucked at their teeth.

"Dude, gross." She pulled the girl away from the table and into the kitchen. "Girl, you're gonna have to get better at being mean. You want me to take him? You can have whatever tip he leaves."

"If he leaves a tip. No, I got it. Fia, look, that's just how it is around here sometimes. You put up with it, or they don't tip. Or worse, they complain, and Ted cuts your hours."

Fia narrowed her eyes. "I'm keeping an eye on him."

The man's group was the only one in the place. Fia positioned herself behind the counter, making sure he knew she could see him.

"Fia. Can I see you in my office?" Ted's gravelly voice leached into the room through the office door before the diner owner himself followed. His leathery skin and the dull gray along his hairline betrayed his age.

"Not right now, huh? I wanna keep an eye on Poe."

Ted snorted. "What are you gonna do, little girl? You're half his size. My office, now."

She pulled herself away from her sentry post and followed him into the closet he called an office. He ushered her through the door with a hand on her back. She turned as she crossed the threshold, backing the rest of the way into the room, refusing to let him get behind her again.

As he pushed the door closed, she opened her mouth to protest, but he cut her off. "I'm sure you've heard how things work around here by now, right?" Before she could answer, he advanced on her, pinning her to the desk.

She shoved against his chest, fighting for room to escape. He grinned, baring predatory yellowed teeth. "I do like it when you new girls try to fight back." He slid sweaty palms up the backs of her thighs, raising the already-too-short skirt above her hips.

Fia's stomach flipped, and she swallowed hard as her lunch threatened to escape. With one hand, she worked to keep him away from the waistband of her underwear. With the other, she used his distraction to her advantage and felt around the desk for a weapon. When she found what she was looking for, she jerked a foot off the floor, driving her knee between his legs, and swung the heavy steel stapler. With a crunch, it connected with his skull, sending him staggering into a chair.

She shoved past him, back out into the dining room, stripping off her apron and slamming it down on the counter. She grabbed Poe by the hand on her way through. "C'mon, we're outta here."

Poe wrenched her arm away from Fia. "We—I can't."

The girl's refusal to leave drove Fia's temperature even higher, until she thought she might actually catch fire.

"Poe! Ted just—"

She waved her hand toward the office door, wondering why he

hadn't followed her out. She hadn't hit him hard enough to knock him out. Had she?

"He's a creep." She was shouting, drawing the attention of Poe's table of grunts, the kitchen staff, and a table of middle-aged ladies who had come in while Fia was in the office. She didn't care. "He pushed me against the desk and hiked up my skirt."

"Fia." Poe's voice was soft and resigned. "I know."

"Know what?"

"I know about him."

With that, Fia put all the pieces together. Ted, the construction workers, Poe's broken acceptance of *how it is around here.*

"Did he put his hands . . . ?"

Before she could finish, he emerged, rubbing a hand over his bruised skull. He stopped short when he saw Fia and Poe.

A low growl formed in Fia's chest, before building to a dragon roar. Poe reached up to stop her, but Fia pushed her aside and charged at the man. He tried to sidestep, but he hesitated a beat too long and she slammed her slight frame low into his torso, driving him back into the kitchen. She screamed again, an animal sound of defiance, and plunged both their arms into the fryer.

"Fia!" Poe shrieked, racing to her side. She pulled Fia off the man and dragged her out the back door.

Outside, Poe pushed Fia down the alley, away from the diner. "Those ladies called the cops when you started freaking out." She pulled Fia toward an opening between two fences. "In here." Poe pushed her forward into the narrow space and reached for Fia's arm. "These uniforms gotta go. I know a place—but first we need to do something about this arm."

Fia looked down at their hands: Poe's unmarred flesh, spotted with cinnamon freckles, and her own, red and blistered. *That should hurt more than it does.* Her heart pounded in her ears and at the edges of her vision.

"Sure, but what are you—"

Poe's crystal-blue eyes shone in the dwindling late afternoon sun, wet with tears. Fia stared in stunned silence, wondering what had suddenly broken the girl who had been so calm up to this point. Poe let herself sob, and hot tears flowed freely onto Fia's melted flesh. Fia ground her teeth at the introduction of salt to the wound—*Now* that *hurts!*—and jerked the limb back.

"What the hell?"

Poe nodded toward the arm. "Look. I think it burned too long. It's going to scar."

Fia held her burned arm up to look at it. It was red and the skin had boiled, but it was healed, mostly. The scars forming looked like scales. *Dragon scales.*

"What the hell?" she repeated, this time with less venom.

"It's a thing I do. C'mon."

"Yeah, sure. Lead the way."

They wound through alleys until they came to the back of a small concrete building. "She'll have clothes for us in here." Poe rapped three times on a green wooden door. Fia took stock of their surroundings. All the windows of the neighboring structures had steel grates covering them. Broken asphalt and gravel covered the ground several hundred feet in all directions, with only the spare weed forcing its way through a crack here and there.

The door opened, and a late-middle-aged hippie woman stepped out, embracing Poe and beckoning Fia forward. Between her patchwork broomstick skirt, flowing tunic, and head scarf, Fia determined she was wearing every color of the spectrum in at least half the patterns of the world. Stripes, checks, floral, and paisley were all represented. Her hair beneath the Moroccan-patterned scarf fell in dreadlocks to her waist. Her black feet were bare and lined with gray-white callouses.

"Beautiful Poe," she cooed. "Who is your friend?"

"Zari, this is Fia."

Fia extended her right hand, and Zari reached for it tenderly.

"*M'amie*! Your hand! Poe, did you tend to your friend?"

"I did. But not soon enough."

"Ah, well, our scars tell our stories, *n'est-ce pas*? I wager there is a good one here."

"She burned it protecting me. Zari, we need clothes."

Zari looked the girls over, head to toe. "And a place to hide, I would imagine. Those sirens are for you, *n'est-ce pas*? Come in, *mes amies*, come in." She stepped aside, ushering the teens through the door.

Inside, the smell of peppers flooded Fia's senses. She wiped at the corners of her mouth, suddenly hyperaware of how hungry she was.

"I will have green chili stew ready soon," Zari said, seeming to read Fia's mind.

Or maybe she just caught her drooling.

"I do hope you will stay and eat."

"Tortillas?" Poe asked, her eyes bright with anticipation. "Zari makes her own." The change in Poe's demeanor—from panicked control to innocent excitement—was tangible and told Fia that Zari herself, and not just her home, was a safe zone.

Zari pulled Poe in close and kissed her forehead. "Of course, *m'amie*. Fia, *belle*, you will stay?"

"Yeah, yes. Sounds delicious." She thought the same could be said if Zari told her she was boiling a shoe. Fia hugged her complaining gut.

After they finished eating, Zari returned to the kitchen, and Fia scooted her chair nearer to Poe. "How long have you been living in the streets?"

"My sister and I ran away about a year and a half ago. Seventeen months and twelve days. You?"

"Not long. About four months. Your sister?"

"Parker. She's a musician. Busker, most of the time. Sometimes they let her play in bars. We're twins."

"Parker and Poe. Cute. Mom liked books, then?" Fia didn't let Poe answer before pushing forward. "Twins, huh? So, can she . . . do the thing . . . ?" Fia waved her scarred hand for reference.

"No. She doesn't even know I can. Or maybe she can, and I don't know."

"You . . . you healed me. With . . ."

Poe waited a second before answering. "Tears, yeah. Like phoenix tears. They heal. About the only thing I can't do is revive the dead." She turned her gentle face toward her lap.

"There's a scar there."

Poe nodded, a heavy sigh shaking her shoulders.

"Hey, it's cool. I got stories too." Fia leaned back in the chair, out of Poe's personal space.

Zari returned from the kitchen. It was a tiny apartment in the back of Zari's crystal shop. The ground floor was comprised of a tiny kitchen with an ancient wood-burning stove, a multipurpose living and dining room, and a room with a toilet. Fia didn't think it even qualified as an actual bathroom.

"Are you sleeping here, *mes amies*?"

"Fia?" Poe studied her face. Fia nodded.

"Good. I was hoping you would." Zari disappeared again, returning seconds later with a stack of blankets. "The bedrooms are downstairs. It gets cold." She led them down a wrought-iron spiral staircase. "My room. Your room."

She pushed the second door open, revealing what had clearly once been a room for children. The walls were a soft green, and a dusty blue valance covered the tiny window at the ceiling. A rocking chair Fia guessed was handmade from a dark hardwood sat in one corner, draped with a quilt in as many colors and patterns as Zari's clothing.

Opposite the chair stood a set of bunk beds in the same dark wood. Poe climbed to the top and peeked over the edge. "Sorry, Fia. Parker always takes the top." She winked, the tension of the afternoon all but forgotten in the moment.

Fia smiled. "No, it's cool. I'm good with whatever." She sat on the edge of the lower bunk, and Zari split the pile of blankets in two, half for Poe, half for Fia.

"Rest well, *mes amies*." She pulled the door closed behind her.

When she was sure Poe was asleep, Fia sneaked out of the room and back down the hall. At the top of the stairs, she turned toward the door.

"I am sorry to see you go, *ma belle*."

Fia started and turned in the direction of the voice. Zari sat in a rocking chair, a twin to the one Fia had left downstairs. A single candle threw deep shadows across her already dark face. Fia struggled to find a response, but Zari spoke again before she needed to.

"I won't stop you. But please, before you leave, come sit a moment with me."

"Yeah, okay." Fia crossed the dark room and took a seat in a plush armchair.

"You have had a turbulent life."

Turbulent. Interesting way of putting it. "I guess."

"You are doing well?"

Fia cocked an eyebrow at the woman. "I . . . guess?"

"You have left everything behind, *oui*?"

"Not revolutionary. Sounds like Poe did too."

"Poe runs to protect her sister, and her sister her. You run to protect yourself."

Fia studied the woman's face. Poe had neglected to tell her that Zari was a psychic. Or a medium. Whatever they liked to be called. Not that Fia was completely convinced. It wasn't hard to guess. A street rat brings another street rat to your door, you know her story before she tells it.

Still, something was prickling the hair on Fia's unmarked arm.

"Demons. You are hunted. But you walked away. Stole out in the dark of night. I tell you, it is not that easy, *ma chére*."

Fia shot to her feet and moved away from the woman, horrified and angry at the legitimacy of her words.

"They will hunt you, Fiammetta, regardless of whether you hunt them. Will you follow me back downstairs? I wish to show you something."

"How—I never told you my name." She searched her memory; she was pretty sure she hadn't told Poe, either.

"Will you come with me?" Zari stood and extended a hand.

Fia reluctantly placed her scarred hand in Zari's, and they retreated down the iron staircase. Zari led Fia into her own bedroom and flipped on the light, revealing deep-red walls covered with protective sigils in a red barely perceptible against the base color.

Fia's breath caught in her throat. Sister Agnes had chosen blues. Sister Marguerite had chosen a sunflower yellow to match her disposition. But there was no question what she was looking at. Zari was part of a world Fia had tried to leave behind.

Fia reached her scarred arm across her chest, touching numb fingers to a similar symbol that had been drawn into the flesh of her shoulder with the thorn of a rose. She let her other hand drift over Zari's wall. Even in the cold basement room, the sigils were warm. Not warm enough to emit their own heat, but as she laid her palm flat against one, she could feel its shape in her flesh.

"I could feel it when you entered the house, Fia. I could feel the energy of the demons following you. They will follow you for the rest of your life."

"You were a nun?"

"No, *m'amie*, I was a hunter, like you. Although I think I was nothing like you. You are strong, Fiammetta, stronger maybe than anyone I've known."

"I am not a hunter."

Zari touched a gentle hand to Fia's shoulder, guiding her to a chair in the corner of the small, dark room, and then sat on the bed facing her. "You were groomed by the nuns, taught their ways. You are . . . seventeen?" Fia nodded. "But you have aged within the convent. Your soul is, at the same time, both young and old. You have learned things about the world most people will never learn, but maybe not many things everyone else knows in their teens."

"They enrolled all the orphans in public school."

Zari curled up the corners of her mouth. "That is some kind of an education, for sure." She leaned her head back against the wall. "I learned my lessons in a very different way." Her voice carried a sad sort of nostalgia, and Fia watched as Zari let her mind wander, to completely leave the room. Maybe even the continent.

Moments later, Zari returned golden eyes to meet Fia's. "How much do you know? How much did they teach you in the convent? Were you told how it all started?"

"Probably not. I'm sure the Church has its own version of the story, right?"

Zari nodded. "Truly, it is only Irzelen who knows the full, accurate tale. And to hear it from his lips . . . well, I am not sure any mortal has."

"Isr . . . ?" Fia tried to repeat the name back to Zari, letting it trail off when she realized she had failed.

"Irzelen. That is but one name given to the beast of Hell—Hades, Gehenna—all accurate and wrong at the same time. It is Irzelen who was charged with governance over a region designated for the ruthlessly violent."

Fia chewed on this a moment. The nuns had never given that particular devil—demon?—a proper name. Or any kind of story. Zari was right about one thing—public school *had* been some kind of education, inadvertently teaching her to question rather than accept blindly. The secrets the nuns had kept were part of the reason she left.

"Honestly, I don't think I know much of anything. I know I hunt damned souls—was trained to hunt damned souls—that don't belong on Earth. I think the nuns might have glossed over a few details."

"Do not blame them, Fiammetta. They could only teach what they know. Do you have a weapon?"

"I was trained on a crossbow, but I left it behind."

"As you would, in order to leave that world behind. But that world is this world. You may ignore it, but it will not ignore you." She paused, letting Fia digest before speaking again. "As I said, I will not stop you from leaving. Please know I'm here."

Fia had been determined to light out into the darkness, unseen and easily forgotten. But now, she hesitated. There was a soft, warm bed across the hall, and she imagined Zari would make breakfast for her and Poe in the morning. But she didn't want to be drawn back into the world she had left, and Zari was part of that world.

"Why did you leave, *ma chére*?"

"I guess I was jealous of the things the other kids talked about: college, careers."

"A pitfall of integrating with those on the outside. You are learning, I think, that you are not meant for that life." She gestured to the fresh scars, a reminder of Fia's rash impulse to protect another human.

They sat in silence a few moments more—Fia staring at her scars, Zari watching her—before Fia found her feet, thanked her hostess, and made her way out of the bedroom and back into the streets.

It wasn't until she had reached the nearest train platform that she remembered: her train pass was in the pocket of the ruffled apron she had thrown down on the diner counter. She swore, stuffed her hands into the pockets of the jeans Zari had given her, and sulked off the platform. She followed the tracks until it was easier to cut through alleys and yards, destined for where she would sleep that night.

It was a small community, mostly runaways, that had taken up in the hulk of an old warehouse. In the short time Fia had been there, she had learned most of the rules.

Keep to yourself.

Keep your hands to yourself.

No drugs.

No stealing.

She had managed to scrape up a couch, a hideous thing with avocado-green and mustard-yellow threads woven through the upholstery, into which she had built a small storage space to stash the few belongings she had taken from the convent. As she approached her couch, her breath caught in her throat.

It was wrapped in an old fabric flour sack, but she could still make out its shape. Lying on her sofa was a crossbow.

She refused to touch it.

That weapon was a loaded syringe. Nothing positive could come of picking it up.

"I was a hunter."

Zari had spoken in the past tense, even after telling Fia it wasn't as easy as walking away. She thought of the child's room, frozen in time. What had it cost Zari to walk away? Fia almost wished she hadn't left the woman's home. Zari might have answers to the questions the nuns had left.

She stared at the veiled weapon a while longer—how long, she wasn't sure—until someone touched her shoulder and she nearly leaped out of her own skin.

The boy was abnormally tall and thin, with dirty glasses and a warm, genuine smile. He called himself Zeke, and he occupied a tepee a few feet from Fia's couch. He'd learned to build them in another life, and he swore that was one of the only valuable things he'd brought with him. How to build a functional tepee and how to field dress game animals—though around here, that was mostly pigeons.

"Christ, Fia!" He clutched his heart dramatically.

"What is it, Zeke?" Fia asked, unimpressed by his performance.

He frowned, disappointed by her lack of amusement. "Some guy left that for you—priest's collar, the whole show. I didn't know you were Catholic."

"Neither did I. What did he look like?"

Zeke shrugged. "Tall. Taller than me, lanky, all arms and legs. Mostly unexceptional."

"Aside from having at least one spider in his ancestry."

"And his nose. More of a beak than a nose."

"Okay, then. Flamingo." She'd been in contact with a handful of priests in the convent. This didn't sound like any of them. "Did he say anything?"

"Nah. Just dropped that there like he knew what he was doing. I thought about taking it inside but wasn't sure when you'd be back. So I put it in the sack. Oh, and I think . . ." He fished around under the cushions of the couch and produced an envelope. "Yeah, he tucked this in here."

She eyed the envelope, skeptical of what she would find inside. It felt like a trap. Zeke pushed it toward her. "Personally, I'd want to see what was in it."

It was a plain manila envelope, large enough to hold full sheets of paper, unfolded, and there was something else inside. Taking care to keep her scarred hand out of sight behind her hip, she pinched at the bulk with the other. The idea that it might be cash intrigued her. It also intensified the feeling that this was a trap.

"Feels like cash," Zeke offered.

"Yeah . . ." She could use a bundle of cash. Even if it was singles, it would be enough for a hot meal.

Or a new train pass.

"Damn it!" she exclaimed, startling Zeke a second time. "I left my tips in that apron too!"

"What apron? What happened to your hand?"

"It's a long story." She'd lived a week in the last twenty-four hours.

"I can't imagine anything but."

Realizing she'd lost close to a hundred dollars between her train pass and tips pushed her over the edge. Though her logical mind screamed in protest, she snatched the envelope from Zeke's hand, opened it, and peeked inside to find a small packet of papers and a stack of fifty-dollar bills, still sporting the currency strap.

She pulled out the money and fanned it against her cheek, breathing in its hypnotic scent. She looked at the strap. "Five thousand dollars."

"Some random priest just gave you five thousand dollars? Why am I not Catholic?"

"I don't think 'gave' is entirely accurate."

She pulled the papers from the envelope. At the top of the first page was a photo. A middle-aged man with close-cropped hair the same rusted red as her own stared back at her. She skimmed over the page: Jameson McLahren drove a bus for the city and lived in Koreatown. Married, no children.

The second page was where things got interesting. Three days earlier, during the second shift she'd worked for Ted, a city bus full of passengers had been found off Colfax Avenue, on the eastern edge of the city, headed out into the prairies.

Or rather, a bus full of dead bodies. They had suffocated inside the bus. The gas pedal had been weighted down with a concrete block and the steering wheel locked in place. The biggest question facing authorities was how the driver had been able to rig the bus without any of the passengers noticing. And where he had gone. The passengers had been found in their seats, with no visible signs of panic or struggle. The bus had simply run out of gas.

Whoever had put together this packet knew the answer to at least one of those questions. There were maps, surveillance photos, itineraries. She didn't think there was anything she could possibly need to find this guy that wasn't in the envelope.

"Shit." Just like that, the world she had tried to leave behind was laid out before her in black and white.

And green.

She hadn't realized this life came with so much cash. She wondered how often it came with this much cash.

There was a handwritten note in the envelope.

Miss Drake,

I have heard a great deal about you, including your attempt to step away from a mission to which you are naturally suited. I do hope that, with this payment, I can convince you to reconsider. Enclosed, you will find information regarding your target, who has been possessed by the ancient soul of a condemned man, as well as where to find the containment collar you will need when you take him down. You will receive the rest of your fee upon completion.

While I respect your choice to walk away from this world, I do hope you will reconsider. From what I've heard, you have the makings of a supreme hunter.

In either case, please accept the down payment and weapon as a gift.

The note was unsigned. She stuffed it back into the envelope and picked up the weapon.

Fia Drake set up a makeshift sniper's nest on the roof of a parking structure in the upper downtown area. There was a bus yard across the street. The information packet the priest had left suggested this would be the easiest place to find Jameson McLahren alone and isolated.

"If you can avoid it, never take down a target in public." Sister Agnes's voice, raspy from years of shouting, echoed in Fia's mind. *"You'll need to move quickly. You only have a few minutes to get the collar on before the soul is released."*

She looked at the collar. It looked simple enough. It was made of metal but was incredibly lightweight and virtually indestructible. On the inside, a copper rod stuck out an inch from the smooth surface. That, she remembered, needed to go into the wound in the neck. The copper would stimulate the nervous system, keeping the soul anchored to the host. A locking closure, opposite the rod, featured a GPS switch that alerted . . .

She wasn't sure. That was probably part of the training she had skipped out on. *Someone* would come and exorcise the soul back to Hell. She imagined a small army of priests, dressed conspicuously in embroidered chasubles and sweeping robes that covered their feet, moving in unison to descend upon the body.

She set up her nest, positioning the bow to fire at the back gate of the bus yard. The yellow glow of nearby streetlamps cast deep, long shadows, and she felt a wave of doubt flood her senses. She couldn't identify a person in the dark! What was she doing up here?

Before the gremlins could lock onto her mind, Jameson

McLahren's face caught the light and Sister Agnes's voice returned to her. *"Account for distance and wind. Aim high to accommodate for arc."* Fia did as she had been told, aiming for his nose instead of his Adam's apple, her true target.

A deep breath in. Out. In. On the second exhale, the bowstring sang in her ear, and Jameson McLahren crumpled to the pavement. She grabbed the collar and ran down the stairs to the next level of the garage. On this level, she thought she could drop through the garage's open center to the levels below.

At least, she hoped she could. It would shave off precious seconds in getting to the street.

Unless she fell and broke her leg.

She threaded her thin frame between the safety rails and dropped down a level.

Two more to go.

Once on the ground, she darted across the street to where she'd downed her mark. She breathed a heavy sigh, strangely relieved to find him still there, still broken, still dead. She pulled her bolt out the way it had gone in. The air around the body—and the body, for that matter—buzzed like a severe summer storm. He smelled stale, like a wet dog. Like a wet dog in the late fall.

She reached out with the collar in both hands. The pavement surrounding Jameson McLahren's head shone wet with blood in the eerie light. She maneuvered the collar around his neck, fitting the copper rod into the wound in his spine. With a ratcheting click, it locked into place, and a green light next to the closure blinked on.

She hesitated, resting on her haunches. She half expected the man to gasp back to life; the other half expected to turn and find ten police cruisers and officers with their guns on her. Several accelerated heartbeats later, none of that came. She straightened her knees and slowly, deliberately, turned away from the collared man, her job here finished.

On the train south back to the camp, she let her head fall against the seat, feeling the ruddy ends of her hair brush against her collar.

Maybe tomorrow, she'd use the bounty to get a real haircut. Or buy a coat. Maybe one for Zeke too.

Zari had been right. Of course she had been. Fia had somehow known all along it wasn't as easy as just walking away. She knew too much. The demons, the souls—they would be there whether she hunted them or not.

She could go back to the convent. Sister Marguerite would smooth things over with Sister Agnes and the Mother Superior. She could finish her training—

Why?

This hadn't been hard. Not as hard as she had expected, anyway. Maybe Zari, the priest, maybe they were right. Maybe she was made for this. And it was sure to get easier, right? She'd develop tricks, strategies.

By the time she reached camp, she'd made up her mind. As badly as she wanted to get far away from nuns and priests and condemned souls, the money smelled good. The adrenaline felt good.

Just another couple bounties, she thought. *Just enough to get me off the streets.*

As she approached her sofa, Zeke's voice drifted from inside his tepee. "Your priest was here while you were gone." He pushed an envelope through the front flap.

Inside, she found not one but two stacks of fifty-dollar bills and information on another bounty. "Maybe a year," she whispered. "You can do anything for a year."

The Crier

Amanda Salmon

"Are you finished sulking? And don't bother telling me you haven't been."

"What do you want, Ashryn?" Lyrial asked, not moving from her perch halfway up the dead tree. Her black hair and clothes blended with the bark. Only her pale skin distinguished her as a separate being.

"I'm here to help, if you're done with useless emotional outbursts."

Lyrial regarded the girl on horseback. "How do you—"

"You wouldn't be *here*," interrupted Ashryn, "if something hadn't gone wrong."

All elves shunned the cursed tree. They were afraid of being tainted by the dark magic that stained it. No one understood why Lyrial chose such a cold and unforgiving place as a refuge. She refused to explain that the tree called to her. If she were to admit that, then she would have to confess her true abilities.

"How much do you know?"

"Your failed mission is no longer a secret, nor are the terms Alrith set."

Lyrial groaned. Her first solo mission as an ascendant had become a shambles. She had scoured the Forest of Moonlight, but instead of recovering the star-kissed ore, she had discovered sabotage. Two other ascendants had usurped her mission.

Apprising Commander Alrith of the situation had been a mistake. He'd goaded Lyrial into demanding another chance to prove herself. He'd offered only one option: she was to find more of the ore. If she failed again, she would be finished. There would be no ascension to the guardians, the elite mages who protected the Elven realm.

Unfortunately, the forest had been the last known location of the ore.

"How could you possibly help? All the ore has been found."

A wicked smile played on Ashryn's lips. "Not all of it."

"What do you mean?" Lyrial leaned forward, casting Ashryn a skeptical look. The girl exuded warmth, from the rosy glow of her skin to the golden highlights glinting in her reddish-brown hair. She radiated sunlight, so the smile did not fit.

"Come out of the tree," Ashryn insisted.

Lyrial rolled her eyes. The rough scratch of bark infused her with comfort as she deftly scampered down. At the bottom, she maintained the physical connection, drawing strength from the small spark of life she could still sense in the heart of the tree.

"Tell me."

"There's a secret stash of ore in a cave in the mountains."

"That isn't vague at all." Lyrial folded her arms. She would need more information, unless . . .

"Wait, this isn't one of your uncle's tales, is it?"

"No. I overheard Thessalin and Eldrine. They plan to raid the cave."

Lyrial scowled. Robbing her once in the forest was not enough? Now they were planning to steal her chance at redemption too?

"Why are they doing this?"

"Do you truly not know?" Ashryn asked disbelievingly. Lyrial did not deign to respond, but her stony countenance demanded an answer. "The spot you took in the ascendants was meant for Ayen—

Thessalin and Eldrine's best friend. Alrith's son. They want you gone so he can take your place."

Lyrial paced, absorbing the information. The burden of an unfulfilled promise settled uncomfortably in her chest. It had been her mother's dying wish for Lyrial to become a guardian. Lyrial had resolved to use every fiber of her being, every trace of her magic, to make that wish come true. No petty jealousy was going to stand in her way.

"When do they plan to raid the cave?"

"Two days. If we leave now, we can reach it first."

"We?"

"I'm coming with you."

"No."

"I wasn't asking for your permission."

"Good, because you don't have it." Lyrial turned and strode away.

"Lyrial!" Ashryn nudged her horse into a trot. She caught up to Lyrial and blocked her path.

"Why do you want to go?"

"It'll be an adventure."

"No." Lyrial skirted the horse and rider.

"There's only one problem with that." She paused, then continued impishly. "You don't know where you're going."

Lyrial grumbled at their slow pace. This was the fourth time they'd stopped so Ashryn could consult the map. Lyrial pinched the bridge of her nose, closed her eyes, and took a long, deep breath. She exhaled slowly. It did not help.

"Give me the map," she snapped.

"Not this again." Ashryn lowered the map to glare at Lyrial. "We've discussed how you have no authority over me. I will not comply with your demands."

"Ashryn, at the rate we're going, Thessalin and Eldrine will get there first."

"Nonsense."

"Any time you think we have, we don't." Lyrial waited. Ashryn ignored her. "Is there a reason you don't want me to see the map? Are we lost?"

"We are not lost. Are you always this impatient?"

"I have to find the ore first. We do not have time to waste," she said fiercely.

Ashryn bit her lip. "Will you make me a promise?"

"What?"

"Promise you won't leave me behind. One look, and you won't need me."

Lyrial waded through Ashryn's words. She weighed the meaning of each and was at a loss. She repressed the urge to lash out, but some of her magic escaped anyway. The temperature dropped, causing Ashryn to shiver.

"I'm keeping the map," Ashryn said.

"Do what you think necessary." Lyrial met Ashryn's warm brown eyes with her own cold blue. "You may have bribed your way into this, but you are a part of it now. I will not leave you. Map or no map."

"Oh," Ashryn said. "Here." She thrust the parchment at Lyrial. Lyrial did not take it. "We're going to the Schadowen Steorra."

"Then let's get moving."

Lyrial urged her horse up the incline. It refused to go. The Schadowen Forest covered the bottom half of the steorra. The trees cast long shadows, perpetuating an endless twilight. Lyrial was determined to not spend another night under the oppressive canopy. Her horse, however, was not cooperating.

She surveyed the area, but nothing seemed amiss. She tugged the reins to the side. The horse eagerly accepted the new direction—the completely wrong direction. She stopped. They'd have to go on foot.

Lyrial dismounted. She worked her shoulders to dislodge the

heavy foreboding that had settled there. Ashryn threw herself from the saddle and immediately dug into her supplies.

"Slow down," Lyrial admonished. "We'll have to walk."

"Why?" Ashryn asked, buckling her sword belt. "It's right there."

Warning tingles cascaded down Lyrial's spine. Her body stiffened in alertness. A cave was visible. It had materialized in the side of a mountain that hadn't been there moments before.

"Hold on," Lyrial said. She checked her own equipment to buy time. This needed careful consideration.

"Ready?" Ashryn tossed over her shoulder as she sauntered toward the entrance.

Lyrial spun around to gauge her progress. The cave was a swirling vortex of shadows mixed with a darker haze of black mist. Ashryn was too close. Hands formed in the mist, reaching for her.

"No!" Lyrial screamed. She flung her arm up, fingers stretched out, but it was too late. Ashryn disappeared into the vortex.

Lyrial dropped her arm. Fierce determination hardened her expression. She strode into the shadows. Prepared for groping fingers, she was taken aback when nothing happened. No pushing, no pulling. The dim lighting displayed a normal cave. The scent of dry earth filled her nostrils. An overwhelming dread spoke of wrongness.

"We have to leave," Lyrial said.

"But—"

"Now!" Lyrial clamped a hand on Ashryn's arm.

The cave plunged into darkness. Ashryn screamed. Lyrial cursed herself for being rash. It was drilled into the ascendants: *use your magic; that's why you have it.*

"Lyrial?" Ashryn murmured.

Lyrial tightened her grip. "I'm here." She focused her magic, drawing it to her senses. She blinked and adjusted to the ice light overlaying her vision. The cave was illuminated in shades of white tinged with the palest blue.

Lyrial looked around, searching for the opening. "Where is it?" she muttered. "It should be right here." Two steps in meant two steps out, but the entrance was gone. The trail of their footprints through the dirt was cut off by solid rock.

A small spark fizzled, drawing Lyrial's attention. Ashryn stood trembling with her eyes squeezed shut. One hand was clenched in a fist, the other slightly cupped.

A flare of gold shimmered in Ashryn's belly. Lyrial watched as it climbed her chest, flowed into her arm, and blazed in her palm. Her rigid stance relaxed. She shifted her hand, releasing the flame into the air. The orb floated above them, providing light.

"What's missing?" Ashryn asked.

"The way out."

"What is this place?"

Lyrial hesitated, not wanting to voice her suspicions. "It's a labyrinth." As if waiting for her confession, a rumbling heralded the opening of a passage. The pair stared into the darkness.

"We're going in there, aren't we?" Ashryn asked.

"It's our only choice."

"I don't like it."

"We're still going."

The fireball bobbed ahead, lighting the way. Lyrial used her magically enhanced senses to scout.

"Do you want my sword?" Ashryn jutted her hip, offering the blade. "I haven't mastered wielding a sword while summoning fire."

Lyrial shook her head. She brought her hands up, crossing her arms over chest to form an X. Then she threw her hands down sharply.

"Whoa!" exclaimed Ashryn. Two ice blades rested in Lyrial's hands. She lifted the short swords. The blades gleamed dangerously sharp.

"Let's go," Lyrial said.

They moved cautiously. They treated each curve and bend like a trap. The dry, earthy smell gradually changed to the aroma of damp earth as they moved deeper underground. Lyrial's magic didn't alert her to anything beyond a tinge of unease or a ripple of dread.

The narrow passage widened. Ashryn stopped. "Do you hear that?" She cocked her head to capture the sound. "Something is coming." The fireball wavered, almost extinguishing.

Lyrial listened. She detected nothing.

"It's a soft hissing sound. It's barely there. It's like—"

Ashryn's breath caught. The fire flickered, blazed, and then died.

"Ashryn!" Lyrial shouted. A blast of fire erupted beside her. She flinched away from the heat, but Ashryn released flame after flame.

"They're everywhere!" screamed Ashryn. "They won't stop."

"Who?"

"Look out!" Ashryn warned. Lyrial dove as flames soared over her head. She rolled and came up on one knee, still clutching her blades. A crazed gleam shone in Ashryn's eyes.

"You have to stop!" Lyrial yelled.

Ashryn turned in a slow circle, flames pouring from her fingers. A ring of fire encased her. Lyrial scuttled back as Ashryn was obscured by the inferno. Lyrial vanished her blades and summoned her ice. The fire hissed and crackled. Steam misted the cave. The air grew thick and damp. Lyrial carved a path to Ashryn.

"Stop," Ashryn pleaded. Sweat glistened on her skin, mixing with tears. "You can't put out the fire. No matter how many I burn, they keep coming."

"What keeps coming?"

"The spiders."

"There are no spiders."

Ashryn's lips trembled. She glanced helplessly around her. "They are everywhere."

"Do you trust me?" Lyrial asked. She grabbed Ashryn's hands. A loud hiss and a puff of steam escaped as ice met fire.

"Please don't." Ashryn's whole body quivered.

"Do you trust me?" Lyrial repeated. Ashryn nodded. "There are no spiders." Lyrial stared hard into Ashryn's eyes. Ice blue clashed with crazed brown. The gleam slowly faded.

"No spiders?" whimpered Ashryn.

"Not a single one."

Ashryn closed her eyes. She inhaled and exhaled, then leaned into Lyrial. "You're doing that thing, aren't you?"

Lyrial chuckled. "Yes." "That thing" was how Ashryn described Lyrial's ice sight.

"When I open my eyes, what am I going to see?"

"The illusion should be broken, but I'm not sure." Lyrial wished she was further along in her training. Then she would have known how to share her sight with Ashryn.

"An illusion? That was an illusion?"

"Yes. A labyrinth is a trap. It will use whatever it can to keep us here."

"There will be more of those things?"

"Yes." *Or worse,* Lyrial added silently.

"I really don't like this place."

Lyrial laughed again. Exhaling a wisp of icy air, she let go of Ashryn's hands and flexed her red, stiff fingers. "We have to keep going. The only way out is through the maze."

Ashryn didn't move. Shadows lengthened, threatening to swallow them.

"We're going to need light," Lyrial added.

Ashryn straightened her shoulders and opened her eyes. A fireball was quickly launched into the air. She nodded. Lyrial conjured her blades, and they marched on.

"Those scoundrels!" Ashryn snarled. "They sent us here."

"We need to focus on getting out."

"I'll focus all right. I'll focus on revenge."

Lyrial didn't argue. Anger was good for banishing fear. The cave led them down dark, twisting corridors. Ashryn stayed close to Lyrial, often asking if something was real or not.

"Do you see the snakes?" There were no snakes.

"The rocks are falling! We'll be crushed." There were no rocks.

"Will you teach me how to do that?"

"As soon as we're out of here."

"Stop!" Ashryn yanked Lyrial backward.

"Ow!"

"You were about to walk off the ledge."

"No, I wasn't." Lyrial jerked free, and Ashryn gaped at her. There was nothing beneath Lyrial's feet!

"Come on," Lyrial said.

On and on it went. Ashryn's revenge was becoming more inventive with each illusion. Disembowelment and castration ranked high on her list. She tried to manifest calm determination, but her nerves were frayed. No matter what Lyrial said, the illusions seemed real to her.

"Is the lake real?"

"No." Lyrial stepped into the black water. Ashryn stifled a scream as a bloated purple hand broke the surface.

"There's something in the water!"

Lyrial turned around. "There is no water."

More and more body parts surfaced. Dead white eyes stared from severed heads. Tattered clothes clung to the bodies. A stray piece of fabric brushed Lyrial's arm. Ashryn shuddered as her fear conquered her anger.

"I'm not going in there."

Lyrial came back. "Close your eyes. I'll lead you through." She placed Ashryn's hand on her shoulder. They stumbled into a rhythm. Images of dead things flashed through Ashryn's mind. Phantom touches hurried her steps. Her toes scraped Lyrial's heels.

"We're almost across."

Ashryn didn't open her eyes. If she did, she would succumb to the illusion. She would drown and become one of them. She squeezed her eyelids shut and tightened her grip on Lyrial's shoulder.

"We're going to have to crawl."

Ashryn was forced to open her eyes. The passage had narrowed on all sides, forming a tunnel. She sent her orb through and dropped to her hands and knees. A welcoming golden glow waited for them on the other side.

Lyrial crouched beside her. "I'll go first. Wait here. I'll signal if it's safe."

Ashryn started to protest, but Lyrial ducked inside. The lake called to Ashryn. It beseeched her to join the dead. The dancing reflections promised escape from the labyrinth. She wouldn't have to be afraid. She would have peace. One step back was all she needed to take.

Ashryn shook her head to dispel the allure. The pull of the lake increased. It no longer pleaded; it demanded. She was one of them. She needed to come home.

"Come through," Lyrial announced.

The spell shattered. Ashryn dove into the tunnel. As she emerged, she gratefully accepted the hand Lyrial offered her. The coolness of Lyrial's touch reassured her.

"Is this real?" Golden coins, glittering jewels, and other treasures were piled throughout the cavern.

"I don't know." Lyrial's ice sight was gone. She blinked, adjusting to ordinary vision. Her magic had been blocked.

"Pretty," Ashryn said, ogling a strand of pearls. Lyrial tracked her as she moved from one heap of treasure to another. "Over here!" She reached for a shield.

Lyrial slapped Ashryn's hand away. "Don't touch anything!"

"But look." Ashryn pointed. Nestled under the shield, a mound of star-kissed ore rested against a wooden chest.

"It doesn't matter," Lyrial said.

"How can you say that?" asked Ashryn, bewildered.

Lyrial wrapped her fingers around Ashryn's arm. "This is a dragon's hoard," she whispered. Ashryn gasped. "We're going to leave everything exactly where it is."

"A wise choice," a guttural voice rumbled.

Lyrial froze. Her hand clenched reflexively, causing Ashryn to whimper. Ashryn in turn scrabbled for Lyrial's arm, and they clung to each other. Slowly, they turned to face the master of the labyrinth.

The dragon was enormous. The tops of their heads came to his knee. His dingy gray scales glinted dully in the firelight. He lowered his massive head. One red-rimmed gray eye glowered at them.

"Hello, little elves. It is rude not to offer a greeting."

"Hello," Lyrial piped. Ashryn squeaked.

"It is a rare treat to have visitors." He bobbed his head at them. "You'll be tasty morsels. Nice tender meat." He gnashed his teeth.

Ashryn emitted another high-pitched squeal, and her nails dug into Lyrial's arm. The pain helped Lyrial think. She ravaged her memories.

"Wait," she begged. A remnant of a history lesson surfaced. "We have traversed your labyrinth and request safe passage."

"My labyrinth?" The dragon snorted. Smoke puffed from his nostrils. "This abomination is no creation of mine." His tail swished. The barbs dug long furrows into the dirt.

"Who controls it?" Lyrial asked.

The dragon huffed, and warm air wafted over them. He sniffed. His eyes came closer. He gazed into Lyrial. Then he laughed, a great, big barrel laugh.

"I will not eat you." Relief enveloped Lyrial, though it was quickly replaced with dread at his next words. "You will free me from this cursed place."

Lyrial waited for further instructions. The dragon, however, was done. "GO!"

The roar jolted their systems. Lyrial jumped, and Ashryn's nails scraped her arm raw. They ran until the dragon's guffaws were a distant echo. A shallow alcove afforded them some respite.

"He . . . let . . . us . . . go?" Ashryn asked, wheezing.

"Not exactly." Lyrial panted. She rocked back on her heels, clutching a stitch in her side.

"That isn't an answer." Lyrial began to speak, but Ashryn held up a hand. "I don't want to know. The look on your face tells me I don't want to know but you're going to tell me anyway. Just give me a minute." Ashryn braced her back against the rock and slid down.

Tongue in cheek, Lyrial paced, waiting for the theatrics to finish. At a gesture, she spoke. "The dragon didn't let us go. He allowed us to leave so we could do his bidding. The only way to free him is to defeat the creator of the labyrinth."

"Do we have to free him? Couldn't we just find our way out?"

"No," Lyrial said "The dragon bound us to him with a quest. We won't be free until he is."

"You are joking." Ashryn studied Lyrial's face, but her expression didn't change. "Of course you aren't." Ashryn fidgeted, dusting off her clothes. "Let me get this straight. We have to find the master of this torture maze. Then we have to defeat them. And we have no clue how to do either of those things. But we do know this mysterious entity is capable of imprisoning a dragon."

"Yes."

"That's just dandy. Do you have a plan?"

"We find the master."

"And?"

"That's all I've got." Lyrial helped her friend into a standing position. "We're near the end."

"That's not as comforting as you think."

Lyrial agreed. They were missing a vital piece of the puzzle. Why did the dragon believe they could free him? Dragons possessed the most potent magic. It was an ancient power. He should not be a prisoner. It did not bode well for the two of them.

Lyrial's magic surged as a wooden door suddenly appeared in the middle of the passage.

"How civilized," Ashryn snarked.

Ten steps, and they were at the door. It swung open in invitation. They stepped inside. Torches set in wall brackets flared to life, one by one. They were in a grand hall. The walls and floor were smooth stone.

"I suppose you're going to tell me those ghosts are an illusion?"

"Oh, no, those are real," Lyrial answered absently. The hall was filled with hundreds of floating apparitions. "Wandering spirits or lost souls. They should be harmless."

"They are lost, but not harmless," a voice boomed. A rush of air parted the crowd. A clear path led to a cloaked figure perched on a throne. He beckoned them.

Lyrial pulled Ashryn close. "Do not touch anything. Keep your fire inside."

Lyrial's magic warned her of deception. The cloaked figure was not the master of this labyrinth. Her senses were drawn to an old peasant man cowering by the throne. The peasant's image flickered. Her ice sight couldn't fix a lucid picture of him.

"Enough whispering," the cloaked figure said. He banged his staff against the floor. A wave of power washed through the room. As one, the ghosts turned to the elves. Ashryn faltered, but Lyrial held firm. They approached the dais.

"Don't bother requesting safe passage. I will not grant it. The dragon's stench is all over you. What lies has he been telling?"

"None," Lyrial said. The dragon had not lied to them. He may have omitted things, but he had told no lies.

"He bid you free him?"

Lyrial nodded.

"It is his way. It will do you no good to listen to him. His confinement is the punishment for his crimes. The dragon elders deemed it so."

"If we don't free him," Ashryn said, finding her voice, "may we have safe passage?"

"No. You are bound to him. Your punishment will be the same as his. You shall dwell here for eternity."

"Why are we being punished?" Ashryn blurted out.

"Because you dared step foot within this labyrinth."

"But—"

"ENOUGH!" he bellowed. "The time for questions is over." The throne and figure vanished.

The old man waved cheerily at Lyrial. She lunged for him, but Ashryn fumbled the attempt. He bared his teeth in an evil grin and brushed a finger against the nearest ghost. Malevolent energy pulsed through it, infecting the others. Silent shrieks morphed their faces into demented horrors.

"Stand back!" Lyrial ordered. She conjured her blades. This time, a thin black vein ran through the ice. She sliced through the specters, and they faded from existence. Lyrial slashed and hacked, carving an apparition-free zone. Then she thrust her blades into Ashryn's hands.

"Keep them back!"

Lyrial didn't have long. Already, water droplets spattered the ground at Ashryn's feet. Lyrial created a ring of frost. The ghosts flocked to the circle, but they couldn't enter it. However, the protection spell was a delaying tactic, not a solution.

The missing piece finally clicked. The dragon's magic would be useless against the dead. No wonder he had laughed. He had recognized Lyrial's true essence.

She made her decision.

"If they break the circle, use your fire."

"You said not to, and what will you be doing?"

"I need time to focus."

"Are you kidding me?"

Lyrial didn't respond. She centered her magic. She reached deep into the well of ice within her. At the bottom, she continued to dig. She searched for those powers gifted to her by her mother. The ones born of death. The ones that could capture a soul.

The powers of a crier.

She wound the magic around her like armor. The ghosts would no longer be a threat to her. They were innocent souls trapped in an endless limbo infected by another's evil.

A fireball whizzed through the air, dispersing the ghosts.

"They won't hurt us."

"How do you know that?" Ashryn asked. She held another orb poised to fly, but a gentle push on her arm urged her to desist. She looked at Lyrial. Her fire dissipated. Lyrial's eyes were no longer brilliant blue. They were ice white.

"Are you . . . can you . . . ?"

"Not now."

Ashryn couldn't believe it. Lyrial was a crier, a mage born of ice and death.

"I'm done with this place," Lyrial announced. "Cover your ears."

Ashryn complied, fascinated. Never before had she witnessed the powers of a crier. Lyrial parted her lips. Pale blue light shot through with white coalesced in her mouth. An otherworldly scream echoed through the labyrinth. The muffled sound reverberated through Ashryn.

"Stop!"

The old man revealed his true form. He loomed from the darkness. Tendrils of shadow clung to him, transforming into a swirling robe. His skeletal frame had the barest covering of skin. Black holes appeared where his eyes should have been. The witch wraith grew to his full height, towering over them.

"They are mine," he declared.

"Not anymore." Lyrial flung her hands up. A torrent of snow and ice poured forth. It gathered in a whirlwind around the wraith. He howled as the storm stripped his power, and his terrifying form dwindled to nothing.

The blizzard wasn't done. It raged through the cave, destroying the last vestiges of dark magic. The illusions were wiped away. The spirits were swept into the wind.

The dragon roared. The storm rushed back, lifting Lyrial into the white. Ashryn squinted. The ghosts were dissolving into the churning ice and snow. White strands flowed into Lyrial until the blizzard was gone, and she was left drifting among the stray snowflakes.

Ashryn goggled. Steam rose from her clothes as she released her fire.

"It wasn't enough," Lyrial said. She staggered into Ashryn, grabbing her shirt. "It wasn't enough," she repeated. "We have to stop him."

"The wraith is gone," Ashryn said. The dragon roared again, and Ashryn's muscles constricted as coils of panic engulfed her. She drew her limbs in, making herself as small as possible. "Y-y-you—" She choked. "You want to f-fight the d-dragon?"

"Be ready."

No stealth was needed in approaching the dragon's lair. He was aware and waiting.

"What is the meaning of this?" he hissed. A clinking sound accompanied his words. Lyrial motioned for Ashryn to halt. She entered alone. Chains made of ice bound the dragon, crisscrossing his body.

"You cannot hold me. I will turn you to ash." He growled, discharging a jet of flame. Lyrial stood her ground. The flame encased her but did not burn. "You dare challenge me?" He roared his fury.

"No," Lyrial said. "But we do." A voice made of a hundred different voices issued from Lyrial. The spirits were taking over. She saw through their eyes. She heard their stories. She learned the truth. "You will face us."

The dragon renewed his struggles. "I do not heed the dead."

"You will answer for your treachery."

Flames erupted from the dragon. This time they met ice. The fire spluttered and died. The dragon coughed, unable to summon more. The ice flowed into him, freezing him from the inside out.

"Now!" shouted Lyrial.

Ashryn rushed in. She unleashed her flames upon the dragon's body. Her clean fire purified the dragon. Part of the wraith's story had been true. The elders had judged the dragon guilty, but he had fled his punishment. A sorcerer had found him. They had wreaked havoc until the sorcerer betrayed him. The dragon killed the sorcerer, and the witch wraith had been born.

The wraith had enslaved the dragon, and evil had grown inside the dragon with every dark deed he committed. Only a tiny part of the dragon remained true. The spirits sought that truth. They would hold him accountable. He would spread the darkness no farther. Lyrial was their vessel, and Ashryn their means.

Ashryn's fire burned bright, lighting all the dark, hidden places. The last of the ice melted, taking the shadows with it. Ashryn stumbled on weak legs. She banked her fire and fell to her knees.

Lyrial stood tall in front of the dragon. His scales shone gold. Sparkling silver irises twinkled. He was magnificent.

"You have freed me."

"To make amends," the choir voice rang. "You are bound to this vessel. She will be your redemption."

"So be it."

The souls retreated into the well of Lyrial's magic. She sank to the ground. She shook with exhaustion, but there was one more thing to be done. She sculpted a jar from her ice, and then she cried. Crystal tears tumbled from her eyes. They made soft plinking sounds as they landed. Each glittering crystal contained a soul. She blinked the last tear into the jar. She was hollowed out.

"You must release them," the dragon said.

"Not here. Their prison will not be their resting place."

Lyrial knelt beside the cursed tree. The morning twilight provided the small amount of light she needed. She stroked a desiccated root. She forged a connection, offering hope and solace instead of taking it. The tiny spark came to life.

"Shouldn't we take the ore to Alrith?" Ashryn asked. She had refused to leave the ore, insisting Lyrial needed it. The dragon, Orione, had freely given it, breaking the dragon hoard curse.

"This is more important," Lyrial said. She noticed Orione shuffling. She indicated the cursed tree. "Was this your doing?" He bowed his head. He wouldn't meet her gaze. Having her answer, she said, "It will be your first amends."

Lyrial emptied her ice jar. The crystal souls spilled onto the dry earth, and Orione melted them with a warm breath. Hazy wisps of light rose. They disappeared into the clouds. The small pool of water fed the parched soil. There was a creak, and the spark grew brighter. It was a start.

"Now we go see Alrith."

The dragon landed at the gates of the ascendants' abode amid shouts and cries of alarm. Alrith's voice rose above it all.

"Stand ready." The commander was positioned on the fortifications above the gates. Thessalin and Eldrine flanked him. "What do you seek here, dragon?"

"I've brought the ore as requested," Lyrial replied.

Orione dropped the mound of ore. It struck the ground with a dull thud. The star-kissed ore glinted in the morning sun for all to see. Alrith stared, dumbstruck. Thessalin and Eldrine shrank away from Ashryn's glare. She smiled wickedly at them as she glided a hand along a golden scale.

Lyrial raised her chin and spoke in a clear, carrying voice. "I am an ascendant, and I will be a guardian."

Spirit of the Dragon

E. A. Williams

My mother was an extraordinary woman. She was our hero since, well, forever. Born in the Year of the Dragon, Mary Reinier collected every piece of dragon literature, sculpture, ceramic figurine, and more that she could get her hands on.

She knew everything there was to know about dragons. When my sisters and I were little, Mom's bedtime stories consisted of tall tales of far-off lands, with beautiful maidens, magic, and of course, dragons.

Despite being diagnosed with autoimmune diseases left and right since she was twelve, my sweet mother never let them stand in her way. She worked hard until her work became too much for her body. As an active member of the community, she held high standards, as well as a sense of pride in the community. She taught us to be there for one another and was the first person we called for anything. Even if she was sick in bed, she would dress and come to the help or comfort of friends, neighbors, whomever.

My dear mother was quite the chef. Soups, desserts, and best of all, her turkey. When we were younger, she called us her muses. I can still hear her voice calling, "Kira, Mia, Marissa! My little muses, you are being summoned!" She could make something as mundane as cooking a completely magical experience. Even after moving out, my sisters and I would still go to our parents' for dinner every Sunday. She would still refer to us as her muses, and our childhood would be recreated. It was remarkable.

One cool fall day, when my mother arrived home from the doctor, I was inside her house, waiting. It was supposed to be a big appointment and my father was stuck at work, so I had decided to surprise her with lunch.

She walked through the door looking pale and defeated. My heart sank, and I knew the news wasn't good. When she noticed me sitting in the kitchen with lunch served, she smiled big, stood tall, and set her things on the counter. I had never seen her pick herself up so quickly.

"Kira, dear, what a nice surprise! What are you doing here?" She smiled, walked over, and hugged me so tight, I lost my breath for a moment.

"Dad told me you had an appointment today, and I wanted to have lunch ready for you. I figured you would be tired by the time you got home." I knew concern was written all over my face. I wished I could hide my emotions as well as she did.

"I did have an appointment today; I just love them there. They are so wonderful. I took some oatmeal raisin cookies to the staff. Your dad and I were up half the night making enough. And no, dear, I'm not tired at all. What makes you say that?" Chuckling and pouring tea, she still hadn't regained her color.

"Mom, you're always tired. I know you well enough to know you're wiped out after a long day, or when you're sick. Especially after an appointment." I arched my eyebrow, waiting for her to tell me she was fine.

I took a sip of my soup, her recipe of course. She made it for us every winter or when we got sick. Chicken and dumplings never tasted so good.

"Kira, honey, I'm fine. Just a busy day, is all. After we eat this amazing lunch you made—thank you, by the way; it's delicious—I'm going outside to tend the garden." She patted my hand in reassurance and ate her soup. I could see she was struggling.

When we finished lunch, she went outside while I cleaned up. I could see her through the window, on her knees, gloves on, and trowel in hand. I watched her for only a minute so she could have a few moments alone. I could see she was grieving, heartbroken. I wanted nothing more than to comfort her, but I knew, as soon as I stepped outside and she heard the creaking of the door, she would put it to a halt and say her sniffles were nothing more than allergies. When she was ready, she would tell us. She probably just needed to talk to my dad first. I stayed with her till he got home and made sure she was comfortable before leaving them to their evening.

A few days later, my dad called, asking for my sisters and me to come over for dinner that night. I called my sisters and passed on the news. I had already called them the day of Mom's appointment and let them know to expect something big.

Mia, Marissa, and I gathered on the front porch of our parents' cottage-like farm. I stood frozen for a moment; I could sense the energy of the house was different. Finally gathering courage, I opened the door and went in ahead of my sisters.

"Mom, Dad? We're here!"

The three of us hung up our jackets and walked into the kitchen. It smelled amazing, as always. Mom and Dad scurried about, cooking, and setting the table, dressed in their matching aprons.

My parents were certainly each other's best friend. They had matching everything. Most days, they dressed in coordinating colors, if not alike. They had always been that way—complete nerds and sickeningly in love.

"My girls!" Mom said, coming around the kitchen island to give us big hugs and kisses. Dad came around from the other side, sandwiching us all together. It was good to see my mom had all her color back.

We sat and ate. My parents asked the everyday questions: How was school going? Was I still going for the promotion at work? Had Marissa sold any more of her art? Things like that.

After we'd gone back and forth catching up on daily life, my parents decided to have coffee outside on the deck.

The deck was my mom's favorite spot, outside of the house. It opened onto a wide, open space with beautiful mountain views, trees as far as you could see, and of course, her garden. It was one of the most relaxing places to be. Sometimes, when I had a bad day, I would come home, and Mom and I would sit out there with blankets and warm drinks. I always felt so much better afterward.

Mia, Marissa, and I settled into the swing, sharing a blanket. My parents sat together on the oversized chair across from us.

"Well, girls, your father and I have some news. Kira, I know you suspected something the other day, and I'm sure you've filled your sisters in." My stomach tightened as I nodded. I wished I could be as steady as her hands were around her coffee cup.

"It *was* a big appointment that day. I'm going to have a lot more, along with a new doctor. Girls, I don't know any other way to say this other than to just come out with it. They found cancer. It's called Hodgkin's lymphoma. They say if you're going to get cancer, that's the one to get. There is a high success rate, and we caught it very early. So I should be just fine."

Mom's expression changed as shock lit up our own faces. She set her cup down and gathered us all in her arms. "Oh, girls, I wish I could tell you not to worry, but I know you will do that anyway."

We were speechless. Growing up with a sick parent was one thing, but she was already physically weak. I had no idea how she was going to find the strength to fight this. I didn't know how I was going to find the strength to accept it.

It was getting pretty cool outside. Through all our tears, as well as lots of sniffles and questions, we all went back inside, and my dad started the fireplace. I dug out all the movies we used to watch together whenever the seasons changed. Fall was our favorite season, but that year, it was just depressing.

That night, we all snuggled up and watched movie after movie. We made a big pallet on the living room floor, and all five of us slept next to each other all night long.

Throughout the following weeks, my father, sisters, and I took turns going with Mom to her doctor appointments. No one wanted her to be left alone. I learned to find my strength in her. She never felt sorry for herself, and she never allowed it to stop her.

She still took goodies to the staff every appointment. Always homemade sweets. My sisters and I would help her with the baking. God only knew how much time we had left with her.

In her home library, she had dragon figurines everywhere. Every shelf was filled with dragons that had some meaning tied to them. When she was stuck in the hospital for weeks at a time, we would take some of her figurines and books to her. Her face lit up each time one of the doctors or nurses asked about them. She would read them the lore and share her stories.

She would go down to the children's wing every day to read to them, to tell the stories she had told us as children. I decided to start recording her voice telling these stories. I wanted to make a book of them for my sisters and me.

The children loved when she came, and they knew that two o'clock sharp every afternoon was story time. They would group together, sitting and waiting. Mrs. Mary's story time was the highlight of their day.

After six weeks of being cooped up in the hospital, she was able to come home. I knew she was feeling the effects of the chemo. She slept more often, and she lost weight, an unfortunate side effect of throwing her guts up nonstop. Although she tried, she just couldn't hide her illness when there was always someone there with her. She still got up to clean, cook, and make sure my dad was taken care of, though. She was the strongest woman I ever knew.

She reminded me of the dragons in her stories. One story came to mind of the Dragon Queen. In her human form, she was a strong, exceptional ruler. In times of battle, she was the one who led the way in her true dragon form. Queen Atauamae was beloved by everyone around her because she was all things good and she welcomed everyone with open arms. She was a fierce protector and would shield her men from harm with her mighty wings.

That was my mother.

My sisters and I took turns helping around the house every night to make sure Dad wasn't overwhelmed and Mom wasn't overdoing it. I loved being a fly on the wall, watching them interact. Marissa had become obsessed with taking photos. She took candid shots of Mom with everyone. They were truly incredible.

My dad would bring Mom trays filled with her favorite tea or coffee. He would set her up in the living room, hand her the remote, tuck her in on the couch, and then they would watch a show, talk, or read together. When Mom was too tired to read, Dad read to her. A few times, I saw him carry her upstairs to their room or just around the house so she wouldn't get too tired. I hoped my sisters and I would all be lucky enough to find a man like my father.

Spring was around the corner when Mom started regaining her strength. She was up and about more often, and the gray hue of her skin began to give way to the beautiful olive complexion she had had before.

I saw my mom in the greenhouse preparing all the seeds and soil for planting. Every year, my mom had a "Welcome to Spring" party. We all brought our favorite spring dishes, dressed in gardening garb, and tended the land. We pulled weeds and planted seeds and new bulbs. Then we drank tea, ate, laughed, and enjoyed each other's company after a hard day's work.

We all pitched in a bit more that year to help make sure Mom stayed off her feet as much as possible.

That year, like every other, was a complete success. I surprised my mom with the book of her dragon tales. I gifted a copy to each of my sisters as well. I also had one made for the hospital, to donate to the children's ward in her honor.

Moved to tears, she stood and hugged me. She held *Spirit of the Dragon* in her arms, smelling the pages.

After the sun set, we begged Mom to read us a story. We all felt like little girls again. Dad made a fire in the pit, and we all sat around as Mom, seated on a pillow, cracked open the cover. Reading the dedication, she started crying again.

"To our mother, Mary. You have been our dragon, our protector, our love. Your stories have brought magic and happiness to so many. We cannot thank you enough."

Marissa did the cover art, and it was beautiful. She had painted an image of our mother with the spirit of a dragon coming out from within her. One of the photos Marissa had taken before Mom lost her hair was placed at the back of the book.

She looked stunning.

Mia, who was still in college at that time, had connections for printing and binding, and she had brought the whole project to life. It really did turn out amazing.

"What story shall I read, my little muses?" Mom asked, overwhelmed by emotion.

"The dragon's poem!" we all exclaimed.

"All right, girls. 'Ode to Dragons' it is." Mom smiled as she turned pages beautifully illustrated by both Mia and Marissa.

"Dragons.
Many see us a winged fright;
we fly, we circle, we protect till morning light.
Sleep solid during the day,
yet spirit alert, watching you at play.
Time tests loyal and true,
courageous, fearless, unstoppable too.

We shake out our wings at night
and fly guard as you sleep tight.
When you pass by and catch sight
of the stony beast that looks awry, don't sigh.
Never hide in fear
for we love you, my dear."

My mother closed the book, grinning as we clapped. My sisters and I had loved that poem since we were little. Listening to her read it once more brought us all back to those days. Mom read a few more poems and stories before we went inside for the night.

By the beginning of summer, Mom had finished her chemo, but it had taken a toll on her kidneys, and she went back into the hospital for transplant surgery. We all were tested for donation, and surprisingly the best match was our dad. He willingly gave her one of his kidneys, and both their surgeries were a success.

When the doctors finally allowed my mom to roam the halls, the first place she went was to see the kids. The nurses announced to the children that Mrs. Mary was coming for a visit.

After story time, my mom made sure to sign the book, as did the three of us. She set it up at a table, and each child had their picture taken with my mom and signed the blank pages at the back of the book. Then she handed out a stuffed dragon to each child. I know it made their day, and it certainly made hers.

Once we returned to her room, she laid down to sleep and stayed that way for a good six hours. She was exhausted. When my dad came in to "relieve" me, I showed him all the pictures. I had taken pictures of the book too since it was to stay in the ward. She had wanted to make sure that any child who came in would get to sign the book.

"If the pages run out, just paste in more," she had told the nurse.

Fall came around once again, one year after the diagnosis, and Mom hit remission! My dad healed completely from surgery, as did Mom. She no longer had to go through chemo. Her hair grew back in beautifully. Where before her hair had been thick, straight, and chestnut brown, now it was thicker, curly, and a deep auburn.

My mom continued volunteering at the hospital for story time with the kids. She started participating in walks for cancer and became more of an advocate for cancer and autoimmune disorders.

Finally, it was time for our annual harvest party, which we hadn't done the previous year due to Mom's diagnosis. Wonderful fall foods, harvested fruits and vegetables, bonfires, and spooky stories. My sisters and I always made each celebration a slumber party. It just made the time more special.

Thanksgiving came, and it was one to remember. The whole family cooked in the kitchen together. As we got ready for our turkey day, we played backyard football and watched the Thanksgiving Day Parade. It was by far the best Thanksgiving we had ever had.

Mom had always had a zest for life, and after the last year, she lived every day as if it were her last. She taught us all to live that way. Who knew that something so tragic could make everyone happier?

After dinner, we took turns sharing what we were thankful for. The one thing we were all thankful for was that Mom was still with us. Once the kitchen was cleaned, we put on our jackets, Dad grabbed the ax, and we all walked down to the edge of the farm to chop down a tree. (We always planted two trees each spring in place of the one we cut down the winter before. It was a never-ending Christmas tree forest.)

Once back inside, Dad started a fire in the fireplace, and Mom made her famous hot chocolate as we began to trim the tree. I put on some Christmas tunes to really get us in the mood for the holiday transition.

Dad brought the lights up to the roof, and Mom, stubborn as ever, climbed up to help. My sisters and I stood on the lawn, watching nervously. I understood my mom felt better and was getting back to her normal self, but it still made my nerves stand on end.

Christmas was always the most special holiday in our family. We decorated our entire tree farm. The whole house, inside and out, was completely decorated. Mom even crafted a new tree topper that year. And not just a normal run-of-the-mill angel for the top of the tree, either. It was a *winter* dragon, as she called it.

It was beautiful. It was made of iridescent crystals that looked like white pearl, with big blue eyes, and she attached white feathers to the wings. In its own way, it looked angelic. The tree had dragon ornaments, along with all the ones we had made as children.

After a nice long night's rest, we had a pajama day. We drank coffee in front of the fire and watched all the classic Christmas movies. I noticed my mom seemed a little uncomfortable. I thought she might have just overdone it the day before. She didn't complain, but she did excuse herself frequently.

On Christmas Eve, we went caroling in town. Afterward, we drove around, looking at the Christmas lights. Mom and Dad sat in the front seat. My sisters and I sat in the back, snuggled together as we oohed and aahed over the lights.

We ended at church for a midnight service. It was just beautiful. When my sisters and I were little, we all would often fall asleep well before the service was over. Mom, Dad, and someone else from the congregation had always carried us to the car.

Once back at my parents' house, I went outside on the deck and brushed the snow from the chair. Everything just glistened—a beautiful winter wonderland in our own backyard. Mom brought out a blanket and sat down beside me, putting her arm around my shoulders.

"You know, I am the luckiest woman alive," she said to me. "I have you and your sisters and your father. And look, we live in this picture-perfect magical land. Nothing could be more perfect than right now."

My mom smiled, kissed me on the forehead, and we sat together watching the stars until we nearly fell asleep.

Then came Christmas morning! Mia, Marissa, and I all ran downstairs like we were five again. We rushed to the tree and patiently waited for the go-ahead to start opening gifts. We knew Dad was already downstairs since the fire was roaring and the smell of brewing coffee and freshly baked cinnamon rolls wafted through the air.

Not saying a word, Dad went back upstairs rather quickly with some ginger ale. I asked my sisters to go ahead and serve up breakfast and coffee for everyone while I sneaked upstairs.

I quietly went into my parents' room, where their bed was in disarray and the bathroom door shut. The first thing my mom always did when they woke up was make the bed. I lightly tapped on the bathroom door, and my dad slowly cracked it open.

"She's okay. I think she just overdid it. She's taking a bath, and we will be down in just a few minutes.

My dad kissed my cheek and shut the door. I had to dry the tears that started to well up in my eyes. I didn't want my sisters to see that anything might be wrong. We had to enjoy this day together. I told myself I could worry later.

I descended the stairs and saw my sisters bundled up together, cups close to their mouths as they laughed and talked. I swallowed the lump in my throat and smiled at them.

"Mom and Dad will be down soon. Is there a cup for me?" I asked while crawling under the blankets they had piled everywhere. Mia handed me a cup, and we sat in silence, admiring the tree.

When we heard footsteps, we looked at the staircase. Two sets of slippers came down, and we threw off the blankets. Mia and Marissa each grabbed a cup of coffee for our parents as they met them at the bottom of the staircase.

"Mom! Are you okay?" Mia asked.

Mom smiled at her, though she looked *very* pale. We hadn't seen her that pale since she started chemo.

"I'm fine, girls. I think with all the running around in and out of the cold, I probably just picked up a little bug. No need to worry." She took her cup, kissed Mia on the forehead, and sat on the couch in the living room.

Dad propped up the video camera so everything could be recorded and no one had to be out of the picture. He sat beside Mom and placed his hand on her knee. Looking at us, he said, "On your mark, get set . . . *go!*"

The race was on! We scrambled under the tree to divvy up the gifts. After they were all passed out, we each opened one gift at a time, going in a circle so we could all see what everyone got. My parents had certainly spoiled us: a beautiful new camera for Marissa, the best art supplies for Mia, and an impeccable antique typewriter for me with a card attached.

To the new storyteller of the family. Write it all . . .

After opening the gifts and eating breakfast, we all dressed for a snowball fight. My sisters and I ran through snowbanks and made snow angels, while Mom watched from the porch. We then went back inside to prepare dinner.

Having five cooks in the kitchen for Christmas dinner was interesting. The kitchen was huge, but with five people hustling about, it got crowded fast. But it was a good kind of crowded. Dinner was perfect and went on till almost one in the morning. Mom was so tired, she didn't even debate other people cleaning up the kitchen. My sisters and I stayed over another night.

The next day around noon, I went to check on Mom. She had gone upstairs to take a nap three hours before. I found her in bed, still sleeping. When I sat down on the bed beside her, she didn't move. I tried to wake her, but she wouldn't respond. Feeling heat radiate off her, I yelled for my dad.

He gathered her in his arms and told me to grab the keys and start the car. My sisters, hearing the commotion, grabbed their jackets and purses.

Marissa drove with Mia, while I rode with our parents. Along the way, I called Mom's doctor so he could meet us at the emergency room.

They admitted her as soon as we got into the building. She had a temperature of 105 degrees. They accessed her port and started her on fluids, taking labs and placing cold packs around her body.

All we could do was pray. We sat in the lobby of the hospital, calling family. Dad refused to leave Mom's side. Thankfully, they were able to get her temperature down that night, and she woke up. We all gathered in her room.

A bit confused as to how she had gotten to the hospital, Mom asked question after question. Finally, after taking a few sips of water, she looked at my dad, squeezed his hand, and whispered, "The cancer never went away, did it?"

All our hearts broke.

Around two in the morning, the doctor came in with the lab results. He explained that her last labs had shown no trace of cancer. They had thought they had gotten it all. Apparently, they hadn't. It had spread so fast and so extensively, there was nothing else they could do. Her kidneys were failing again, and her body was shutting down.

We were in disbelief; this couldn't be it. Damn cancer! It destroyed not only the person who had it but the lives of those left behind.

My mom was speechless. Tears overflowed her eyes, and she held my father's hand so tightly, her knuckles whitened.

After a few hours, she had digested the news, but we hadn't caught up yet. Knowing I could lose my whole world on any given day was something I couldn't accept.

I asked the doctor, begged him for anything we could try. Bone marrow transplants, another kidney. Anything.

I was devastated and desperate, but the doctor explained that nothing could be done. She wouldn't survive the surgeries.

I went to the hospital chapel to pray. My sisters joined me till my phone rang. It was our dad, asking us to come back to the room.

"Girls, sit down." My mom smiled. "Oh, my muses, I am so sorry. I am sorry to leave you. We knew this was a possibility. It just came sooner than we wanted. I want to go home. I don't want to die in the hospital. I want to be in our home, look out the windows, and be surrounded by just you. How do you feel about that? I don't want to do it if you feel you wouldn't be able to step inside the house again."

My mother was so calm; it was clear she had made her peace.

"No, Mom, it will always be home," Marissa said, her voice choked with emotion. "I'm not saying it won't be hard, but if that's what you want, that's what we will do. I'll start making calls." She got up and stepped out of the room.

After home hospice care was arranged, my sisters and I moved back in. We wanted every second we could get with Mom, and we couldn't let Dad stay there alone. He carried her up and down the stairs as often as she wanted. We could have brought in a bed for downstairs, but she was more comfortable in her own room.

Over the next few weeks, all Mom did was sleep. One night, before she fell asleep, we all said our goodbyes. The nurse was there with us, and we all surrounded Mom in my parents' room. As her breath began to slow, we all placed our hands on her.

I knelt beside the bed. "Mom, your love and strength, courage, and determination has been unreal. You have been our hero. You are the spirit of the dragon. We don't want to let you go, but we will be okay. It's time for you to go fly with your dragons now. We love you so much." I kissed her hand, not yet letting go.

A smile spread across her face, and she hoarsely said: "I love you all too."

She let out her breath and never inhaled again. The nurse checked her vitals and nodded, stepping back. The room erupted in sobs. We all leaned on one another, unable to hold ourselves up. She was gone. Off to fly with her dragons and to watch over us as we slept.

After a couple of hours, the funeral home came for her. As they brought her outside, insects started flying about in hordes. Once I had wiped the tears from my eyes, I saw what they were: hundreds of dragonflies in the dead of winter.

That was my mom, letting us know she was still there with us. That it was all going to be okay. After her funeral, we continued all her traditions. Each time, we were surrounded by dragonflies. Surrounded by our mother's spirit, the spirit of the dragon.

Daughters of the Dragon

G. Pearl Kilgore

The sky burned a brilliant purple. The twin suns of Drayson Three scowled at each other, as though in bitter competition to see which could roast me alive first. Beneath it all, I rattled along the path up Esme's Mountain in an open truck that had seen its best days decades earlier.

The driver had a one-word name: Jessop. His brown face was weathered from a life spent outdoors, and he seemed to wear a permanent film of dust on his clothes.

The truck hit a big bump, and I grabbed for the two cartons lying on the seat between us, each marked with an orange biohazard label. "Easy, Jessop! These are irreplaceable."

"So sorry, Dr. Ferguson! We haven't had a chance yet to repair the road after the winter rains. And we don't have the budget for a hovercraft. You medical people get all the university's funding. No one cares much about ancient geology, ecology, or history when there are people in the here and now to keep alive and well."

I couldn't argue with that. That attitude had been the way of things ever since the first colonists arrived from Earth over two hundred years earlier. But for me, at least, the past was very much relevant to my here and now.

I just hoped we reached our destination on the summit before the contents of the carton thawed in the blazing second-summer afternoon. I wasn't dressed to handle biohazard material, though I did wear gloves, something Jessop had noticed but hadn't acknowledged until my hand slipped from one of the cartons.

"Why not take them off? It's too hot."

"I'll be fine."

I wished I could remove them, though. They were dark tan to match my skin tone and coated with plastic to stay clean. In the scorching heat, they were instruments of torture. Liquid puddled around my fingers, and I would have tossed the gloves aside in a second if I were alone. I expected Jessop to ask why I wore them and was relieved when he didn't. It was a question I had been dodging for over a year, and I wasn't ready to tell him just yet. In truth, he was probably one of the only five hundred thousand people on the entire planet who would understand.

We slowed nearly to a halt as Jessop maneuvered over another rough spot. I held my breath as the truck moved perilously close to the edge of a precipice, but then I forgot the peril as I took in the view. Magdalena City lay far below, a metropolis of fifteen thousand surrounded by a ring of mountains that rose in scarlet splendor to embrace the purple sky. I could see the university's clock tower in the center of the city—an impressive beacon when seen from the ground, it was just a sliver of silver from this height.

"Amazing, isn't it?" Jessop commented. "Just imagine what the Earth colonists must have thought when they saw it two hundred years ago."

"We descend from amazing people," I agreed. "Ten thousand humans voyaged across the stars to a hostile wasteland, adapted themselves to it, and built a civilization. Now here we are. Thanks to scientific advances, we're more fit, have greater endurance, and live longer than they ever did back on Earth. Even our skin makes more melanin than before to protect us from sunburn. We are evolving every day. All of us."

He smiled politely at my enthusiasm. Then he asked another question that followed me everywhere. "Your last name is Ferguson. Are you related to Magdalena Ferguson?"

"No," I said. "It's just coincidence. My first name is Chrysalis. It's some silliness my parents came up with. I wish I were related to her. I would have loved to have known her, to hear about her life with the space program. Exploring beyond Earth's solar system. Sending out the missions that eventually found the Drayson System and saved humanity when the sun began to die."

"You could lie and say you were related," he joked. "If I had that name, I might."

"First, do no harm," I said. "I try to live by that. Are you really a Ferguson, Mr. Only One Name?"

He grinned. "I see what you did. But no, my family has only had first names since the days when my ancestors lived in African tribes. But maybe I'm related in spirit to President Ferguson. You know, Esme is very much like her—brave and strong, even at her age."

"I know. I'm honored she agreed to be part of this project. Her insights, her experience, and of course her, uh . . . medical history . . . and . . ." I faltered as the reality of my research and the need for it returned to the forefront of my mind.

"She's going to die from it," Jessop said regretfully. "You can say it. Everyone close to her knows it, and we've had to accept the inevitable. She's only the fifth person to ever contract Dragon Fever, and no one has ever survived it."

"No, they haven't," I said softly, clenching my hands inside my soggy gloves and fighting an overwhelming urge to cry. An electric spasm of pain screamed through my hands, and they locked into the curled position. I forced my fingers open and flat again. "It's always fatal."

The dire prognosis had been banging away in my own head for over a year. Hepatic Cutaneous Syndrome was the official name, and I was the sixth person to be diagnosed with it. Unless a cure were found, Professor McCoy and I would both die of it.

But a cure required a cause, and so far, there was no known defect, pathogen, or allergen to explain it. There were only guessing and a set of very clear symptoms, including high fevers.

A symptom that decided to manifest itself on that trip up the mountain. I was suddenly burning up and dizzy.

"Help," I gasped. "Too hot."

I was aware of Jessop stopping the truck and giving me something to drink. I was aware of the surprise on his face when he took off my gloves and saw the clawlike curvature of my fingers, the yellow-and-green discoloration around the nail beds, and the distinct golden pattern that looked like scales.

"You have it too," he said. "Are you the only other one?"

I nodded. "No other cases but Professor McCoy's," I said, just before I fell into an uneasy sleep.

The dragon was a magnificent creature as large as a commuter shuttle. Her scales glinted like living emerald and turquoise. Her roar shook the trees. A jet of blue flame nearly singed my hair, but somehow, I wasn't afraid of her.

She tossed her head in invitation and spread out a wing. I climbed aboard, grasping the ruff of orange spines on the back of her neck to hang on. We swooped off the ridge, free-falling toward the rocks below. I screamed, and she roared in answer, then swerved sharply upward, high into the sky.

Just as I thought I would lose my grip, she dove again, straight down at the university clock tower. It bonged in protest as we flew past. Below us, people fled, their faces stricken. Then the dragon climbed high into the sky and made a sharp swerve, and I was falling through the dusty air . . .

In that unsettling way of dreams, I landed with a thud that woke me up. Jessop stood over me, fanning me with his hat. "Dr. Ferguson?"

"I'm not a doctor yet," I answered. "Not completely. Haven't finished all my advanced courses. Too sick."

"Drink this. It helps." He pressed a canteen to my dry lips, and I tasted a strange herbal flavor.

"What is it?"

"Coquille tea. The vines grow all over the mountain. You can't miss them. They have blue flowers that look like seashells. It's the only thing that's really worked for Esme's fevers. She had me bring some along for you. I could also open some of the boxes and get the ice out to bring down your temperature."

In a panic, I scrambled for the biohazard cartons but couldn't find them. "No! Don't touch them! I need them!"

He pointed to the floor. "Safe. What are they, anyway?"

"Blood and tissue samples from the other patients who had Dragon Fever. Some of them have been frozen for two hundred years. You can't imagine the trouble I had getting them. The only reason I managed is because of how far away I'm taking them from the general population."

He nodded with grave acceptance. "We're going to be in quarantine, my husband and I, along with you and Esme. Ari and I haven't been sick, but we're ready to stay with you anyway."

As we got moving again, I said, "I've already been isolated in one way or another since my diagnosis. I have no family left to worry about, so I decided to use it as an opportunity to study this thing, inside and out."

"Why has it taken so long?" he asked. "Why hasn't anyone really studied it in depth before?"

"As you said earlier, the colonists were busy building a civilization. Why waste resources on people who all ended up dying? When the first two victims got sick after arrival, they did go into quarantine, but it didn't spread. Since they happened to be brother and sister, the authorities surmised that it was some kind of allergic reaction to the environment and closed the books. At least they kept the samples.

"When the next two patients got it close to a century later, there was a bigger gap between them. Twenty years, actually. And they weren't related. They lived on opposite sides of the planet from each other. But again, it was ruled a probable allergic reaction."

We reached the summit of the mountain as the first sun began to set. I was aware of two figures exiting a low red-brick building with a domed roof. One of them, a man, ran toward us.

"Jessop! We were about to call for help! Did you get lost?"

"Don't worry, husband of mine." Jessop laughed as he got out of the truck. "I could never get lost. But Dr. Ferguson needs a bed right away. She's feverish."

"I'm not going to bed! I have to take care of these samples and all this equipment! Where is my lab?"

"Go to bed, young lady," I heard a woman say. "I'll see that everything is put away. Gentlemen, kindly step aside so I can see our guest to her room."

According to her files, Esme McCoy was 170 years old and had lived on the mountain most of her life. It had even been named after her. Because of her advanced age—remarkable even by Drayson standards—I had expected her to be small, shrunken, and frail.

But there she stood, tall and fit in the purple twilight, clad in white coveralls that matched her hair. She wore roguish dark glasses, red lip stain, and a crooked smile. Her hands were hidden behind her back, as if she had been caught in the middle of some mischief.

I scrambled to find my gloves, but Esme's words stopped me. "Let me see your hands. I need to confirm that it really is you, Magdalena."

I frowned. "I'm sorry, but I'm Chrys Ferguson. I'm pleased to meet you, but I really need to find my gloves."

"No need to be ashamed here. Let me see your hands."

I reluctantly held them out for inspection. Professor McCoy looked them over and let out a whoop of joy. "Oh, I knew it had to be you! You finally made it!"

"Well, I did get sick along the way, but . . ."

"No, I don't mean that. No. You came home! Finally! I've been waiting forever for you!" Then, as if she were a dancer on a stage, she did a little jig, whipped her hands from behind her back, and yanked off her sunglasses. Then she held out her hands for me to see.

Her fingers were gnarled, the brown skin marked with an unmistakable pattern of golden scales. There was a ring of blue around her pupils, but the rest of the irises were deep gold. It was the second most obvious sign of Dragon Fever, a yellow ring that began on the outermost edge of the iris and worked its way inward, growing wider as the illness progressed. The wider the ring, the less time the victim had left.

She leaned in close and inspected my eyes too. "Just green. No ring yet."

My strength was fading quickly. "Ari," Jessop said urgently. "Can you carry her to her room? I'll start unloading."

"The samples . . ." I protested. "Freeze them right away."

"I'll take them," the professor said, an odd sadness filling her voice. "Poor darlings. All that's left of them. At least the dragons are home now."

Ill as I was, I didn't think much of the words at the time, but they weren't to be the only strange thing she said in the following days. I awoke the next morning to find her sitting on a cot next to me. She offered a glass of deep-blue liquid.

"Coquille tea. It's kept me on my feet since my scales appeared five years ago."

"Five years?" I choked. "You've been symptomatic that long? Your file said your symptoms started two months ago!"

She shrugged. "So I told a fib. I was pretty sure it was nothing contagious since neither Ari, Jessop, nor any of my students got it, and I didn't want some bureaucrat to throw me into quarantine for nothing, so I kept quiet. Like you, I wore gloves at first, which no one questioned since we wear them in the field anyway. Truth be told, I've probably had it longer than five years, but the tea is quite tasty, so I've had gallons of it over the years. I even cultivate my own now. I'm sure you'll want to test it, to see why it helps with the symptoms."

"Yes, I do! No one has ever survived with it this long! You've set a record."

She smiled. "Which means you need to drink up, young lady. Then I'll show you the others. Oh, and please call me Esme. There's no need for the two of us to be formal. Not after all this time."

I didn't point out that we had just met. Instead, I commented, "Others? I thought your students were all gone?"

"You'll see. I'll show you around. Then I'm sure you'll want to get started on your work."

The house was large, built mostly underground. The walls were made of red mud bricks that kept it cool. My room was in the student's dorm. In the center of the house was a great room with a skylight and several seating areas. Beyond that, save for the kitchen and classrooms, every inch of the place was full of shelves. They were everywhere, standing as partitions between rooms and lining the walls, and nearly all of them overflowed with statues of dragons of varying size and configuration.

As it turned out, these were "the others."

"Meet the family," she said proudly. "All of them have found their way back here, and now you have as well."

"So you like dragons, then. I can see why. It's an impressive collection."

Her face fell. "That's all they are to you? Just art?"

I didn't want to hurt her feelings, but I wasn't sure what she wanted from me. "Yes. What else would they be?"

"I don't know, but I hoped you would," she said expectantly. "I just know bits and pieces."

I was at a loss. She was a revered figure in the scientific community, yet she believed the dragon statues were real.

She sniffed. "You should go to your lab now, Magdalena."

"It's Chrys," I said. "Not Magdalena."

She walked away, but I heard her snarl, "I know who you are."

There was no mention of dementia in Professor McCoy's files. Quite the opposite, actually. The records from a few months earlier noted that her mind was remarkably keen. None of the other patients had exhibited mental disorders either, and her confusion worried me.

This could be a new symptom, a sign that Dragon Fever, whatever it really was, had undergone some sort of mutation, which could mean it was caused by a microorganism. Suddenly, my quest had become about much more than finding a cure for myself. If there was some unknown pathogen lurking and it had mutated, every person on the planet was at risk.

The next two months passed with little progress. I analyzed samples from all the patients but couldn't find a common link. Before Dragon Fever, Esme had been very healthy, and her medical records were almost bare. If only she had reported her symptoms earlier, then I might have had a better baseline to work from.

The only thing that showed any progress at all was the coquille plants, which turned out to be highly nutritious and full of anti-inflammatory and antipyretic compounds.

"So I was right," Esme said proudly during one of her visits to the lab. "It helps you too, doesn't it? You haven't had another fever fit since you've been here, have you? And the pain is better now?"

"It is," I said. "I just wish I knew how it all fit together."

"And what about dreams?" she asked, holding one of her statues. "Are you having any of those? You should be by now. I may not know how it all fits together either, but I know that it does. There's too much to be coincidence."

I nodded at the statue in her hands, a red fire dragon. "Have you always liked them? And where do you get them? I've never seen them for sale in stores."

She smiled. "Well, now you're asking the right questions. They came from right here. This one, I found when we were digging the foundation for this house."

"Wait. You're saying someone left them here?"

"Yes. Every single one was found close to this house. It's why I never let my geology students dig here. I don't think the world is ready to face the truth."

"But the twelve planets in the Drayson System were uninhabited," I argued. "Only this one was livable, and the explorers who found it did very detailed scans. There was no sentient life here and no evidence that there ever had been."

"Hmm . . . maybe someone covered their tracks really well, Chrys." She frowned at me. "Are you sure you haven't been having any strange dreams? I used to when I was little. They're what drew me here."

In fact, I had been having dreams, but they weren't the type I ever spoke about. In my freshman year of college, I had gone with my parents to explore a cave. It collapsed, and they were killed. Knowing they had wanted it for me, I stayed in school and kept my grief to myself. But it had visited my dreams, and I often awoke bathed in sweat and tears.

I still had that dream, but it had changed. I now saw the same dragon I had dreamed of on the trip up the mountain. Sometimes, I flew on the dragon's back; sometimes, I was the dragon, and I returned to the cave and reached in with my powerful claws and pulled my parents out just before the rocks fell.

Other times I flew, not through skies of purple lit by two suns, but through a blue sky with one sun. I saw lush green fields instead of dusty red mountains, and I saw my parents alive and well.

Not wanting to encourage Esme's delusions, I kept quiet, even as the dreams became more real. Every morning, I awoke with my hair plastered to my head in dark sweaty strings.

I had gone back to work, barely noticing when Esme left the lab, but then I heard Jessop call me. "We found another statue, and I'm out of solution to soak it in. Can I borrow some?"

I turned around to see him standing in the doorway. "Is it really true? You did find them here?"

"Of course it is. There's something at work here, Chrys, whether you want to face it or not."

"Something at work? Some kind of magic, I suppose?"

"Sometimes magic is just technology we don't understand yet." Then he laughed. "Maybe something like that."

I wanted to scold him, but then I saw him pointing at something in the corner.

"What in . . . how is that even possible?"

Esme had left the red dragon behind when she walked out earlier, setting it down next to one of the petri dishes of samples. The dish was glowing with yellow light.

While I stood there speechless, Jessop ran to find Ari and Esme. I reached out to move the dragon, to see if the glowing would stop. When I touched it, I felt a tingling in my fingers. Then I was pulled into a vision.

I saw a young man, bursting with excitement to finally reach Drayson Three. His only family was his sister. I saw them build a house from the kits the colonists had brought with them and watched as they got sick only three weeks after their arrival. I saw the doctors in their biohazard suits, isolating the patients and trying every medicine they had, all to no avail.

All those things, I had read countless times in the case notes. But there was something else this time, something one doctor said to a colleague as they got ready to preserve the tissue samples.

"Did you ever see a cloud of light around them? It made me think of a nebula, for some reason."

"You mean like an aura?" The other one snorted. "You think some bad energy cloud killed them? We're scientists! We don't believe in magic."

"But I did see something. Not bright, but something."

"You've been without sleep for almost three days. Go home and rest. I'll get someone else to help me."

Esme let out a war whoop when I relayed the vision to her. "Finally!"

"But he was right. How could a cloud kill them? A cloud of what?"

"A good question!" Esme declared. "And this also confirms my theory! Ari, would you mind getting my blue dragon from my room?"

"What's the theory?" I asked.

"You'll see." She grinned mysteriously, and I thought for an instant that the gold rings in her eyes glowed like the petri dish.

Ari placed a hollow blue-glass dragon into her hands. She held it up so everyone had a clear view. Moments later, the scales on her hands glowed gold.

"I knew this one was somehow mine when I found it," she said. "I started seeing things from times long gone. Like stories from different times and places. I saw you many times, Chrys. There were details that kept repeating in different ways, patterns, as if they were put there for me to remember something. But I don't know what.

"I believe, though, that the statues are vessels of memory, somehow connected to us. When I talk about the dragons as being alive, it's because I've seen them that way. They lived here, and they left something for us. I wanted to tell you, but you wouldn't hear it. You thought I was insane. But think of this. What if Dragon Fever was around back then too? What if they left information about it? A cure, even?"

My air of scientific superiority crumbled and died at my feet, and I felt deep shame. I had been sent to help her, but my arrogance had kept me from listening to her. "I'm sorry," I said. "I shouldn't have jumped to conclusions."

"Well, you always were that way," she said with a wave. "Now, let's see if we can find yours, and maybe theirs." She nodded toward the rest of the petri dishes.

Though Esme published her findings on the dragon statues, she omitted pertinent details, knowing that if she spoke of them, her work would be discarded and her reputation destroyed. As I am writing a personal account and not an academic treatise, I will fill in the details she left out.

I have written many academic papers, and perhaps you are reading this now because of my earlier work. If you have read this far, good reader, I hope you will continue, even if this tale takes a turn you're not expecting. Every word of it is true, and by the time this record is made public, I hope enough time will have passed that this information will be accepted.

So, here it is.

Esme's belief was true. We found the other three statues, and each of them revealed bits of the puzzle that had been left for us.

Yes, left.

None of it was accidental, though it took time to sort the pieces into the correct order. My dragon was tucked away in a drawer, where Esme had put it to repair a break. When I held it, I felt as if a piece of me had been missing from my body.

The break, it turned out, was fitting because I lived two lives at once in the next few minutes: One as Chrys Ferguson, and one as a young woman who loved to pilot anything that could fly. There were overlapping facts, such as our ages and our interest in science. The cave-in also happened to both of us. My parents died, but hers lived and were there to give her good news as she recovered in the hospital, along with her friend—a woman with blonde hair and a familiar name stitched onto a flight jacket.

McCoy.

"Magdalena!" she yelled. "You're in! You've been accepted into astronaut training, even though you have a broken leg."

That day at the hospital, her friend left for Magdalena a green-and-turquoise dragon figurine that was small enough to fit into a pocket. "Looks like a great flyer. Thought it would bring you luck. Take it to space with you, if you want."

Magdalena did, carrying the dragon on missions to the outer planets of Earth's solar system, and then beyond. It was in her pocket when she took the oath of office as President of Earth. It was with her in old age when she sent the explorers out into deep space as the sun began to die. It was with her when she saw the first images of the Drayson System, and with her when she closed her eyes the last time.

Through the knowledge stored in the statues, we found an underground chamber in a location I've sworn to keep secret.

Inside, we found definitive proof that the dragons were real: the massive skeleton of a great flying beast. We also found the technology she left behind. Her name was Anklatu the Great, and she was the oldest and wisest of the dragons. She ruled as their queen for centuries and hatched many eggs in a structure that resembled a chrysalis. Two of those eggs hatched at once—two sisters, one blue, one green, who flew together and studied the ancient wisdom of the dragons.

In that chamber with Esme, Ari, and Jessop, I saw them all as they had been millennia before. There were dragons of every shape and description. Water dragons swam in sparkling streams. Fire dragons nested on mountaintops, laid eggs in special cocoons in the rocks, and lit the night skies with their flames. Ice dragons played in fields of snow.

Every one of the statues was there. They spoke. They sang. They lived.

Then disaster struck. There was a supernova far away, but not far enough. Nine of the twelve planets in the Drayson System were wiped clear of life almost instantly. The other three were blasted with radiation so powerful that it forever changed their ecosystems.

The dragons learned how to open wormholes through space and time and to transform into other creatures on habitable worlds. But they needed to find a way back home once the radiation had dissipated. The statues were beacons to help us return.

Anklatu stayed in the cavern for the rest of her life, looking for a way to bring the dragons home again. The cavern provided some shielding, but the radiation eventually killed her and damaged the gateways and equipment. Later, a flash flood scattered the statues, and they were buried by nature and time.

At first, we were able to travel back to the Drayson System, but as the equipment degraded, we became stuck along the timeline or on distant worlds. Some lived on Earth in dragon form until they died. Others transformed into human embryos, returning after death to the spaces between time and lives. Six of us eventually made our way back in human form, but the residue of the radiation was still in the environment. It was harmless to pure humans, but deadly for us. By the time Esme and I arrived, it had dissipated enough that we could live longer than the others.

History remembers me as the last victim of Hepatic Cutaneous Syndrome and the discoverer of Ferguson radiation. I was also part of the team that developed an antidote for the syndrome.

Sadly, we did not find the cure in time to save Esme's life. She died peacefully on her mountain two years after my arrival. In those years, she made many remarkable discoveries, including finding and translating the records that Anklatu left behind. Jessop and Ari were there with her and are credited as codiscoverers. Jessop keeps the old truck going, even though he could afford a whole fleet of hovercraft if he wanted them.

As for me, I left the field of medicine after I was cured. I have other things to do now. I hear them in my dreams, those other dragons who are scattered across the cosmos. If you are reading this account, I am no longer on Drayson Three. I'm somewhere out among the stars on a quest to find my brothers and sisters and bring them home again.

In a World Full of Princesses

Charleigh Brennan

I first met the woman when I was seven years old. My mom had finally decided to let my brothers and me have a cat after she discovered mice in our house. She put out a few queries to find an appropriate cat, and a shelter called us within a few days with a cat that sounded like a good match.

As we drove to the shelter, I imagined a fluffy Persian or a sleek calico that would curl up in my lap for constant cuddles. What we found waiting for us wasn't what I expected at all: a relatively ordinary tabby with half a tail and some fur missing from the top of his nose.

He was perfect.

The shelter worker explained that he had been found by a woman who was eager to see him placed with a loving family. So eager, in fact, that she had come to the shelter in hopes of meeting us.

I sat on the floor, and the cat immediately climbed into my lap and started purring. I'd never felt so immediately connected with an animal before. It was as though we had been destined to meet.

I was so preoccupied with him that I only briefly glanced at the woman who had found the cat when she walked in. I gave her a small smile, then focused my attention back on the cat, who had now moved on to one of my brothers.

I thought very little of the whole interaction. In fact, I only just barely remembered the woman later.

The next time I met her was about a year later. I was in a bookstore with my family, and I was agonizing over choosing a book. I was so distracted, trying to find the perfect book, that I walked straight into her.

"Oh, I'm so sorry," I said, horribly embarrassed.

She gave me a smile so warm that her eyes seemed to shine with kindness. "It's okay. I have those moments sometimes too."

I smiled back and turned to look at the bookshelf in front of me. I began to pull books out at random, in hopes that something would appeal to me. All I could do was sigh as I put each book back where I found it.

"Are you having a hard time finding the right book?" the kind woman asked.

I nodded shyly. I didn't want to talk too much to a stranger, but she seemed so nice that I didn't want to ignore her, either.

"I know a really good one, if you'll let me find it for you," she said.

"You do?" My caution dissolved as I hopped eagerly in response.

She turned back to the bookshelf, scanned the books quickly, and then pulled one out.

"Here it is!" She began to hand me the book, but then pulled it close to her chest and looked me in the eyes. "Before I hand you this book, I want to tell you one thing, and I want you to remember it. Okay?"

I felt a little nervous, but I nodded.

"Okay." She bent down to my level. "I want you to remember this: in a world full of princesses, always be a dragon."

"In a world full of princesses, always be a dragon," I repeated.

"Good. Remember that. Being a princess may be nice, but being a dragon . . ." She paused thoughtfully. "Being fierce and strong and independent is important. It may not mean much to you now, but in the future, you'll find value in it. Okay?"

I nodded again.

"Here you go." She handed me the book, then gave my head a pat and walked away.

I looked at the cover, where a princess wearing a paper bag as a dress faced a dragon. I'd always loved fairy tales and often imagined what it would be like to be a princess. I'd never thought of being a dragon before. It seemed kind of scary. I took her word for it, though, and skipped back through the aisles to find my mom so we could buy the book.

The woman was right. I loved it.

I didn't see her again for a few years. I switched to a new school shortly after meeting the woman the second time, and it was a disaster. I was mercilessly picked on by other kids, and even one of my teachers gave me a hard time, frequently embarrassing me in front of others.

Given, I was an easy target. I was shy and sensitive, and it was easy to get me crying. My dad had died when I was far too young to understand what death was, and I had only just begun to process what that meant. All the heavy feelings seemed to close in on me, stifling my sense of hope.

My only true comfort came from Tau, the cat we had adopted. I'd come home from school and hide in my closet to cry. Somehow, Tau always knew something was wrong and would come find me. A scratch at the door and some soft mewing was his way of telling me he was there. Whenever I let him in, he'd immediately sit in my lap and start to purr. I'd pet him as I cried, gradually releasing the pain in my heart as he comforted me.

Being a single parent, my mom worked so hard that she couldn't see how far I was slipping into grief. Things looked good on the outside. I was a good student, I was quiet, I followed the rules. On the inside, things started to get so bad that I wasn't sure I wanted to live anymore.

Tau was my touchstone. His steady presence kept me from going so far into darkness that I couldn't get back out again.

Unlike everyone else, Tau felt like the perfect embodiment of love. His gentle nature helped me let go of my self-destructive feelings; I loved him too much to leave him behind. That reasoning slowly extended to my family. We'd struggled through so much together. If I took my own life, it would hurt them. I just couldn't do that to them. They didn't deserve it.

After three years at that horrible place, my mom transferred my younger brother, Kaito, and me to a local public school, while my older brother went on to high school. I felt like I had been released from a long prison sentence. However, I was naive to expect that a mere school change would fix everything.

Two days before classes began, my mom took me to my new school to find out Kaito's and my classroom assignments. When we arrived, there were two other girls my age checking the list, which was posted on the wall outside the cafeteria. My mom approached them and started asking questions, much to my horror. My cautious nature was strong by that point, and the last thing I wanted was to have a conversation with two girls I didn't know.

"Hello, girls! What grade are you going to be in?"

They glanced at me, an awkward kid who didn't know how to dress after years of school uniforms, and then traded a look with each other. My mom seemed completely unaware of what that meant, but I knew. They would be nice to my mom's face, but somehow I'd pay for it. Years of being bullied had made me good at picking up those subtle clues.

The pretty one twirled her finger around a strand of long brown hair. "Fifth grade," she said politely. Her smile lit up her green eyes.

Mom, stop talking. Stop talking! I hoped beyond hope that she'd leave it at that.

"Oh, wonderful! This is my daughter, Kaida. She'll be starting fifth grade too. Maybe you can all be friends."

The girls exchanged another subtle look.

Oh, crap. Now you've done it, Mom.

I was going to pay for this. I knew my mom meant to be helpful and kind, but she'd just thrown me back into the lion's den, and I was furious. Those girls definitely didn't want to be my friends, and frankly, I was so embarrassed, I had absolutely no interest in being their friend, either.

I didn't know how it would all play out, though, until the first day of school.

Alphabetically, my last name placed me firmly near the end of the line to walk to class. By the time I found my assigned desk, most of the other kids were already seated. A piece of binder paper sat on my desk, folded and addressed to me in pencil. It didn't look in any way official, so I took a quick glance around to see if there was a sign of who had left it. Of the two girls my mom and I had met, only one was in my class—not the green-eyed one, but the one who seemed to be more a follower than a leader.

I sat down and opened the note.

Dear Kaida,

I don't want to be your friend. I'm not going to tell you who I am now, but I will tell you who I am at the end of the year.

It was decorated with little hearts.

It was the stupidest thing I'd ever read.

I knew full well what bullying looked like. This was the weakest attempt I'd ever seen.

In a world full of princesses, be a dragon.

I'd carried the phrase around with me for so long, but it hit me then what it meant. In the stories, princesses were often cursed or victimized and left to be rescued. Dragons, however, were strong and didn't need anybody. I realized I didn't need someone to fix this for me, and I definitely didn't need approval from either of those girls.

I folded the letter back up, stuffed it in my desk, and started talking to the girl next to me.

By the end of the day, I had made a new friend, successfully avoided those two girls, and stuffed the letter in my backpack to bring home. I was so preoccupied thinking about the letter as I walked home that I wasn't paying full attention. I walked straight into a woman.

"Oh my gosh, I'm so sorry!" I looked down at my feet, blushing furiously.

"Hey, kiddo, how have you been?" replied a vaguely familiar voice.

I looked up and saw familiar chocolaty eyes gazing at me. I took in the woman's warm eyes, her pretty curls, her, well, kind of odd green-and-gray jumpsuit that looked vaguely like it belonged in a science fiction novel. I didn't know her name, but I knew her. It took me a moment to place her, but then I remembered the book.

"*The Paper Bag Princess*?"

She gave me a beautiful smile. "Yeah. Did you like it?"

"Oh, I loved it! I still like to read it, even though I can read much longer books now." I was proud of my love for books.

"Good. How was your day?"

I debated telling her. I usually had a strong sense of stranger danger, but it didn't go off with her. I may not have known her name, but since I had met her before and nothing bad had happened, I decided it would be okay to say something.

"Well, it was my first day of school, and someone left a mean note on my desk." I pulled it out of my backpack and handed it to her.

She looked it over and nodded knowingly. "What do you think about it?"

"Well . . . well, it's mean, but weirdly enough, it only stings a tiny bit. It barely hurts at all."

She smiled sagely. "Have you decided what you're going to do about it?"

"Well, I'm pretty sure I know who wrote it, and I don't want to be her friend anyway, so it kind of doesn't matter, does it?" I paused thoughtfully. "Is that . . . is that the right thing to do? I don't want to be mean, but I don't have to be friends with someone who is mean, do I?"

"Listen, kiddo. It's always good to try to be decent to everyone. However, you don't have to be friends with people who might hurt you. There are always other people in the world who will be better friends. You deserve to have those better friends, and they'll be lucky to have you." She handed the letter back to me.

"So, I don't need to be mean back? I can just find other friends?"

"Exactly. Don't give her any power over you. You'll find other friends." She looked at a watch on her wrist. "I have to go, but I'm glad to see that you're thinking less like a princess and more like a dragon."

"'In a world full of princesses, be a dragon,'" I replied, happy I had remembered.

"You got it, kiddo. See you again someday!" She turned and walked off.

I felt incredibly relieved. I had spent so much time over the past three years letting other people take my power. Not that it was my fault; I hadn't known better. Now . . .

Well, now I could keep my power to myself and only share it with those who were worth my time. Who knew such a dumb letter could end up making me feel so much stronger than I'd ever felt before? When I got home, the first thing I did was tear up the letter, walk over to the garbage can, and throw it away. The girl never told me who she was at the end of the school year, but by that point, it didn't really matter anymore.

A little over a year after the letter incident, I had another quick glimpse of the woman. Kaito and another boy ran to meet me after school. Once they'd reached me, Kaito bounced on his feet in excitement.

"Kaida! Kaida! Can I go to Lanny's house today?"

Lanny put his hands together as if to beg. "Please?"

I didn't want to let them down in their excitement. I really didn't. However, I knew my mom wouldn't want either of us going to anyone's house unless she had met their parents first.

"I'm sorry, guys, but Mom wouldn't like it. She doesn't know your family, Lanny. Come on, Kaito. We need to go home."

"Aw, man," Kaito complained, but he resigned himself to my answer. He then looked at his friend. "Bye, man! I'll see you tomorrow."

Lanny's face went red. Instead of accepting what I had said, he shouted, "Well, at least I still have a father!"

Kaito and I looked at him in shock, then looked at each other. "Bye," we said at the same time, and then we walked together off the school grounds.

Once we were far enough away, I spoke. "That was a really dumb thing he said. He was trying to insult me, but he ended up insulting both of us."

"Yeah," Kaito replied. "That was really dumb. I don't think I want to be his friend anymore."

"I don't think I'd want to be his friend, either," came a familiar voice.

I looked up and saw the woman standing on the corner. She gave us a wave and a wink, mouthed the word "dragon," then walked away.

When we got home, I started thinking about the woman. Who was she, really? She'd never told me her name. All she seemed to do was show up once a year or so, act like my own personal Yoda, then disappear. She didn't seem like a bad person, but what did she want from me? Why did she keep showing up? She was almost like my fairy godmother, except she didn't want to make me a princess. She wanted to make me a dragon. Why?

In middle school, there were a couple of girls I hung out with: Monique and Harper. It was mostly a friendship of convenience. We were in almost all the same classes together, and we were all good students. It was just easy to hang out together.

At least, it seemed that way at first. Over time, as the friendship evolved, it felt less like a friendship and more like a tug of war. The other two girls were competing to be valedictorian when we graduated, and I was stuck in the middle. The more it continued, the more I wondered why I hung out with them.

One day, near the end of eighth grade, I was feeling down. It was the anniversary of my father's death, and for some reason, it was hitting me hard. I couldn't quite figure out why. Maybe it was because, by that point, Tau and all my grandparents had also died around the same time of year. It was all too easy to start spiraling down into that familiar dark, hollow place inside me that I'd fought so hard to climb out of years before.

"You don't seem like yourself," Monique said as we lined up at the end of PE.

"No, I'm not," I said. "I'm really not."

"What's wrong?" She only sounded slightly concerned, like she knew she had to ask but didn't really want to.

I gathered my thoughts. "I think it's because it's the anniversary of my dad's death."

Maybe I was too honest. I knew very well that people had a hard time talking to a kid about losing a parent. It made them uncomfortable. The hardest thing was, when I needed someone to care and help me feel supported, I often felt like I had to take care of them instead because it was hard for them to hear it. They didn't understand that it was even harder for me to live it.

This time was no different.

"I don't want to talk about that. It's too depressing."

I couldn't speak. Now I was not only feeling miserable but also shocked by her lack of compassion. We only had a month left of school, we were going to different high schools, and this was what she decided to say? I realized at that moment how very little I'd come to matter to her. I was just something to argue over with Harper, much like their ongoing competition to be valedictorian. I realized then and there that I was done.

I decided to continue going through the motions with both her and Harper through the end of the school year. It just didn't matter to me anymore. I was going to be free of them. I was going to escape the tower they had placed me in. I'd now emerged from my safe little princess chrysalis; my long dragon wings were ready to spread and fly me to better places.

I was walking home alone, musing over the way Monique had rejected my feelings, when, once again, the woman was there.

"Hey," she said gently.

"Yup," I replied rudely. I continued to walk quickly, my anger fueling my desire to get home.

She caught up to me and started again. "You're having a hard day. Want to talk about it?"

I stopped. "Talk about it? Talk about it? Yeah, right. Because people *really* want to talk about how *I* feel. I spend way too much time listening to other people's problems, but the rare moment I need a friendly ear, nobody wants to hear it."

She put her hands on my shoulders to stop me. "I do want to hear it."

"Yeah, really?" I couldn't hold back my anger or my sarcasm anymore. "Why weren't you there when I was suicidal? Hmm? If you wanted to hear it, if you're such a nice person, why didn't you come to me then?"

"I was with you then. I just couldn't be there physically. That's why you had Tau. I knew I couldn't be there to help you, so I wanted to make sure you had someone who cared."

"And now he's dead too!" I shouted. The dam that had just

barely been holding back all the stress I was carrying finally burst. I started sobbing uncontrollably.

The woman pulled me into a hug. I just kept crying, releasing my feelings as bits and pieces of the figurative dam were swept downstream by the torrent of water forcing its way through.

"It's okay. Just let it out," she said softly as she gently rubbed my back. "You have every right to feel hurt."

After a couple of minutes, the flood of tears trickled to a stop. I pulled off my glasses, now foggy and damp, and cleaned them with the edge of my shirt.

"I'm sorry," I said, my voice thickened by my tears. "It's not really your fault."

"It's not your fault, either. You never asked for all this." She pulled out a tissue and helped me wipe my tears away. "You do have a choice about how you deal with it, though."

"I know, I know. 'In a world full of princesses—'"

"Actually, I wasn't going to say that, but it does apply. You can be the kind of person who waits for others to fix things for you, or you can be the one who sees your struggles as opportunities to grow. You get to choose. You don't have to be a helpless princess and wait for someone to rescue you. You can save yourself. It doesn't mean you have to give up on other people. You just don't have to wait for someone else to make things better."

She pulled back and gave me a smile. It wasn't her usual bright smile, though. I could see pain in her eyes. It was the same familiar pain I'd seen in my own eyes whenever I had a hard day.

I nodded. She'd been through things too. She knew. "Thank you."

"Always." She kissed me on the forehead and stepped back. "I can't guarantee that you'll see me again anytime soon. But we will meet again one day, and it will be a bit of a surprise for you. Once it happens, though, a lot of things will make sense. Just remember that you have something beautiful and unique to offer the world. Never, ever give up on yourself, okay?"

I smiled back at her. "Don't worry. I'll be the dragon."

"Good girl." She gave me a quick hug and then stepped back.

At that point, I was an overweight girl with glasses and braces and practically uncontrollable, frizzy hair. I looked at this beautiful woman with bouncy curls and warm chocolaty eyes. I wished I could be as confident as she was.

She took my hands in hers and gave them a little squeeze. That was when it hit me: there was something familiar about her, and it wasn't just because I'd seen her a few times before. She began to walk away as I tried to figure out what it was. I looked down at my hands, trying to puzzle it out.

"Wait!" I shouted, but when I looked back up, she was already gone.

My teenaged years passed relatively normally—well, normally enough for a girl who looked like the quintessential nerd. Sure, I was picked on by boys who thought it would be fun to catfish the nerdy girl. It was annoying, and I didn't have any good comebacks—I wasn't confident enough yet. However, I could make my excuses or bore them until I was no longer interesting enough to torment.

I mostly hung out alone my first two years of high school. Then I made friends with a transfer student who was just about as nerdy as I was. That friendship expanded into a group of friends. I studied and did fairly well in my classes, had fun doing school plays, and didn't date at all. It wasn't what I thought high school would be, but then, I wasn't taking the princess route, either.

I may have been awkward, and I didn't fit in with the more popular kids, but I was starting to like who I was. That woman was right. I didn't need to be a princess. I could take my own route. I could choose to discover who I was without following the norm. I didn't feel like I was missing out by choosing to be the dragon. I felt like I was on the right path: my own path.

From time to time, I'd vaguely spot the woman out of the corner of my eye. A part of me wanted to run up and hug her, but at that point, I cared more about showing her who I could be.

It wasn't until I started college that I began to notice something a bit odd. By then, my braces had been removed for a couple of years, I'd learned to turn my frizz into curls, and I'd started wearing contact lenses. I would occasionally pass by a mirror or a window and think I had seen the woman, but whenever I turned to look, the image I'd see reflected would only be mine.

Something about that didn't quite sit right, but I tended to shake the thought off and continue on. I decided to get in shape, and after a lot of hard work, I shed the extra weight.

I was at the gym one day when I had that same experience, thinking I'd seen the woman out of the corner of my eye. I turned to look at the mirrored wall and saw myself.

Then it hit me. I dropped the barbell I was using to the floor and walked to the mirror, staring at the image I saw. It was her. It was the woman. I pulled back in shock.

I was the woman.

The realization hit me like a ton of bricks. I put the barbell away, grabbed my stuff from my locker, and ran back to my dorm room. There, I dropped off my things and went to take a shower.

As the water ran over me, I processed everything. I must have traveled back in time to meet my younger self. Why would I do that? She had always been there to support me and remind me to be myself.

I gasped in shock. *That . . . that's it!*

I had once told my mom, when I was about seventeen, that I wished I could go back in time to my younger self and tell her that things would get better. Goosebumps suddenly covered my arms despite the steaming water. I must have actually made that happen!

After that, I switched majors and studied whatever I thought might possibly pertain to time travel. I got my bachelor's degree in physics, then went on to grad school. I fell in love, got married, got a job working for the most off-the-wall scientist I could possibly find who wanted to make a time machine, and then had a daughter.

By the time I was thirty-eight, we'd done it. The first functioning prototype was complete. I went home that night and gave my husband a long, wordless embrace the moment I walked in the door, my heart racing with excitement.

"What is it, love?" Gray asked, obviously surprised by my enthusiasm.

"We did it!" I declared. "I mean, yeah, it's only the prototype, but we did it!"

"That's amazing! Are you going to go back, then?"

I'd long since told him what I was working for. Though I was sure the story had to seem fishy to him, he was just weird enough to accept it. His gaze held a complex mix of emotions: eagerness, curiosity, and a touch of concern. No matter how much he supported this seemingly half-baked scheme, I knew he loved me enough to want me to be safe.

I nodded as my daughter entered the room. Candace was seven years old . . . the same age I had been when my future self first showed up in my life. My heart ached at the thought of what might happen. I had been working for so long, knowing that I'd go back in time, but would I make it back? The future ahead of me, after my time travel, was a complete blank. I'd known what my goal was for so long, but now that it was in sight, I wasn't sure what to do after that.

The expression on my face must have been pretty strange because Candace approached me and offered me her hand. I got on my knees and faced her.

"Mom, what's wrong?"

I sighed. "I have something I need to do, and I don't know how long I'll be gone."

"Is it important?" Candace took both my hands and swung them gently with her own.

"It is." I pulled her into a hug. "I have a special assignment for work, and I'll be leaving tomorrow. I'm going to miss you."

"It's okay, Mom. You'll be back as soon as you can." She pulled back from the hug and gave me a kiss on the cheek. "You know how I know?"

I smiled at my sweet daughter, trying to hold back my tears. "How do you know, sweetheart?"

"Because you're a dragon. You're strong and brave, and you can do anything you put your mind to." She looked up at Gray. "Right, Dad?"

Gray came over and pulled us all into a hug together. "That's right, Candace. Your mom's the most powerful dragon in the world."

I went to work the next day after saying my goodbyes. I might have lingered a little longer than I had to. Even though I knew the task ahead needed to be done, it was still hard to leave my family behind. I was resolute, however, and filled with anticipation as I put on my formfitting green-and-gray hazard suit, making sure I had tissues in one of my zippered pockets.

After a careful check by the launch team, I settled into my seat and strapped myself in. I watched as flames began to lick the sides of the time machine through the windows and listened to the countdown.

I pressed the trigger on one and felt a disorienting surge of energy. I smiled with determination.

"Okay, Kaida. Time to be the dragon."

Seiryuu's Fire

K. T. Seto

"There was a bit of a hiccup, but everything is in place, Ana. They're about to call you in." The admiral's voice reverberated through the communications implant behind my ear. I rubbed my finger over it to adjust the volume, then moved a bit farther from the entrance to the hearing room to ensure privacy.

"Is my cover blown?"

"No, and we'd like to keep it that way. Just try to draw things out a bit; it will take time for us to get a lock on the frequency, if it exists."

He was going out on a limb for me, so I ignored the jab.

"Remember," he continued, "don't tell them until I give the word."

"As if I would."

"Your temper is well-known."

"As is my intelligence," I countered. I ignored the snort of laughter he gave in reply.

"A lethal combination, to be sure. Just use your instincts and be ready for anything."

"Acknowledged."

I pressed the implant to end the call and adjusted the fit of my bodysuit. *Use my instincts.* As if I would do anything else. My instincts told me this would work, and they were rarely wrong.

The doors in front of me opened. I offered a silent prayer to Seiryuu, then walked down a long hallway that opened onto the main chamber. My footsteps echoed in steady counterpoint to the disembodied voice coming from the speakers that lay somewhere near the ceiling of the corridor. The voice's owner was the current joint liaison, Representative Allston, his distinctive Terran accent unmistakable despite the fact I couldn't see him yet.

The Hall of Justice had two formal hearing rooms. This was the larger, with a spectacular view of Luna's capital and seating arranged on either side of a long center aisle that terminated at a raised platform. The committee had segregated itself, Lunar officials on one side, Terran on the other, with a small Martian contingent near the front, possibly attending out of curiosity or obligation.

I'd attended a handful of inquiries here over the past twenty years, but this would be the first where I'd have to discuss an op that hadn't yet reached its conclusion.

Out of habit, I noted the location of the exits as I walked to my seat; there were four, all flanked by upkeep bots and the normal contingent of LPF guards. I saw one bot flash red, instead of blue, in its normal rolling pattern, and slowed. Not upkeep bots, then. Bomb sniffers.

On the dais at the front of the room, the officials sat together at one long table behind Representative Allston, who had a small desk to himself. I scanned the crowd, counting two full teams of agents mixed in among the assistants and DC officials, and rapidly reassessed my position. Suddenly, all my meticulous planning and obsessing over details seemed pointless; bomb sniffers and a second team added too many unknown variables to calculate. Even for me.

Seiryuu's warriors meet fear with fire, I thought, my steps sure despite my momentary uncertainty.

"We have heard the testimony of General Kingston of the Lunar Peace Force and the Terran Anti-Terrorist liaison, Arthur Simon, on the findings of this committee and the quality of the intelligence provided by the Dragon to the Discipline Commission on the existence of a plot to assassinate the prime minister of Luna." Representative Allston nodded to the two men seated facing him at a small conference table. "We will now hear the testimony of Special Agent Muolo of the IIRC, who has information on the events leading up to the tragedy that brings us here today." He nodded in my direction, and a guard instructed me to take the empty chair at the table with the two men.

I mounted the stairs, keeping my hands at my sides and my back straight—projecting confidence as I ignored the sounds of restless movement among the audience. Fixing a calm expression on my face, I sat where instructed. I took a moment to adjust the microphone and move the pitcher of water and glass they'd provided for my use to the side of the table so they wouldn't block my view, then waited for Representative Allston to speak.

"For the record, this hearing is to resolve any conflict that remains in the minds of the ministers and representatives gathered here today, and the proceedings will not alter or impact the conclusions reached by the Discipline Commission and the lawful governing body of Luna."

Representative Allston's voice echoed through the chamber, amplified by a dozen hidden speakers, and based on the amount of eye-rolling I could see, I guessed he was repeating this statement for my benefit.

"Be here advised that any outbursts or personal attacks against Special Agent Muolo will not be tolerated and will result in the expulsion of the offending party from this committee for the duration of these hearings."

He seated himself then with a loud clearing of his throat, and I had to stifle the urge to roll my eyes as well.

"Please state your name and rank for the record."

"Ana Muolo, special agent first class, with the IIRC Joint Terrorism Task Force, Luna Division."

"Agent Muolo, you have been called before this committee to address questions surrounding the deaths of fifteen Terran citizens, the destruction of two Terran living complexes, and the damaging of a Lunar landing facility. Please understand that we are in no way calling into question the rightness of your actions as we—"

"Aren't you?"

My words echoed, and I heard several gasps and chuckles from various spots in the audience. As opening salvos went, I considered that a softball. The splotches of red that rose in Representative Allston's face told me that no one had warned him about me. Sadly, I doubted I would be much nicer as the hearing went on.

"Agent Muolo, I am sure you are aware that there are many who would naturally feel the need for explanations when there has been so much loss of life and so many far-reaching ramifications from an operation as complex as this one."

"Representative Allston, I am a true and loyal daughter of Luna. I will answer whatever questions are deemed necessary by the Discipline Commission according to the guidelines stipulated under section sixteen of IIRC Judiciary Code."

I gave him an insincere smile. Invoking section sixteen meant I could withhold from my testimony anything deemed classified or potentially classified with no penalty. His face flushed again, and I mentally added another point to my imaginary tally.

Representative Allston cleared his throat and looked down at his digipad as if he were gathering his thoughts. He came off as a supercilious little snot, this official liaison between Terran and Lunar forces. I had never worked with him; in fact, I doubted he'd known I was an agent before today, though our paths had often crossed. My undercover status usually kept me off the radar, so to speak.

He cleared his throat again. "Agent Muolo, the general has testified that you provide all the digital support for the Luna Division of the Joint Terrorism Task Force, in addition to occasional field work."

"This is correct."

"What kind of digital support did you provide for the agents on this mission."

"There was only one agent on this mission."

"The agent known as the Dragon?"

I allowed myself a small smile. "That is correct."

His expression clouded. I took a moment to look around the room, gauging the reactions of the people in my line of vision.

"What kind of digital support did you provide the agent on this mission?"

"Very little past the initial insertion." He frowned, and I mentally added another point.

"Agent Muolo, there is a question as to what methods were used before and during the operation. There are rumors that secure databases were hacked and the Dragon committed acts deemed illegal under the IIRC Unified Code of Conduct."

"I am sure this assembly is above entertaining conjecture based on rumors, Representative." I made sure to keep any hint of amusement out of my tone. I heard a few stifled coughs and laughs from the gallery, but I didn't turn to look, instead fixing my gaze on the representative.

"You deny that databases were hacked to create a persona for the Dragon within the Terran military?"

"The methods used to facilitate the completion of missions given to agents of the Joint Terrorism Task Force are deemed classified and are not subject to the UCC under section sixteen. Further, I am not authorized to offer conjecture on this matter."

"Fine. Would you please clarify your previous statement?"

"Which one?"

Another round of stifled coughs filled the chamber, and I leaned back in my chair. I could hear the growing frustration in his voice when he spoke, and it loosened some of the knots my stomach had tied itself into when I'd seen the second team.

"You said you supplied minimal support beyond the insertion. Could you clarify that statement?"

"Yes."

I waited. After ten seconds, I swore I could see smoke building around his ears, but I kept my expression blank. When my communicator vibrated, I reached up as if to tuck back a stray hair. My commander's amused voice sounded after a slight pause.

"We've picked up the signal. It was buried in the scrambling frequency the DC is using for this building. We haven't cracked it yet, but it is definitely going to someone in that room. Keep this going."

I didn't reply as he triggered the automatic disconnect. Representative Allston cleared his throat, his face far redder than it had been when I sat down.

"Agent Muolo, please explain, in detail, your role in the operation on Terra."

I looked around and waited until I had the full attention of the dignitaries on both sides of the audience.

"Once the Dragon infiltrated the base, I kept a detailed account of activities using undetectable surveillance methods, recording all movements and conversations."

I paused, letting the bombshell I'd just dropped penetrate.

"You are testifying here under oath that you saw and heard everything the Dragon did for the entire time he was on Terra undercover."

"This is correct."

"The Dragon's mission report did not indicate your presence, nor did it mention any other agents. We assumed this was redacted."

"The redactions only affected matters deemed sensitive."

"For the record, you are saying that the Dragon worked this op alone and you provided no logistical support after his insertion? That you did not go into the compound with the man known as the Dragon but you saw and heard everything he did?"

"This is correct." I curled my lip but didn't elaborate.

"What you are saying is impossible."

"It is very possible. The Terran government is aware that all Lunar agents are Augments and that we further specialize our genetic manipulations to facilitate our missions, although the full details are classified. Suffice to say, this is entirely possible. Even when we are alone, we are not alone."

I tapped my fingers on the surface of the table, drawing their attention to my hands, inviting them to look at me in my uniform and speculate about what might lie beneath my skin.

"Very well." He nodded. "If what you are saying is true, questioning you would be the same as questioning the Dragon on this matter." He smiled.

The sound of something falling drew my attention to one of the dignitaries at the table behind Representative Allston. Though the man sat with members of the DC, he wasn't one himself; I could tell just by looking at him. I was sure I had seen him before, but I couldn't remember where.

The man wore the gold armbands of the official government regalia on his wrists and a heavy green cloak over a bespoke suit despite the warmth of the conference room. Terrans had body temperatures lower than those of Augments, and the combination triggered my memory. He was the new ambassador to Luna. The Unified Government of Terra had appointed him despite his well-known disdain for Augments.

The look on his face as he stared at me had my instincts humming, arousing the hunter within. Normally, I would try to suppress it, but for some reason, I wanted him to see the predator. Despite his position, he was no friend to Luna, and I was one of her guardians.

"That argument could be made," I said, turning my attention back to Representative Allston.

"Given your previous statement, I move to consider Agent Muolo a material witness and count her testimony as a firsthand account of activities."

I nodded but didn't reply as they seconded and ratified the motion. I kept my gaze fixed on Representative Allston. He was up to something.

"Now then, Agent Muolo. Why did the JTTF target the Colorado compound? Mr. Simon has testified that this particular facility was, at the time, home to approximately four dozen families, including an undisclosed number of children."

My spine stiffened as I realized where he was heading. What insanity lay behind the logic of these bureaucrats? Why feign concern over the methods used to take down terrorists? Clearly the intel was correct: they had no clue about the traitor.

When the operation started two years ago, intelligence stated that a new militant organization called Pure Minds, Pure Bodies had arisen and were responsible for attacks on several medical facilities and tourist areas. It had taken months of research to discover that the PMPB was just an offshoot of the PSG—Pure Species Group, a terrorist organization that had been active on Terra for over a hundred years.

Now we knew why we'd never been able to stomp them out. Someone who had a lot of pull with the Terran government was protecting them. The public outcry when the compound fell had been swift, and it had been utilized by those same terrorists to get themselves onto Luna with the traitor's help. Politics, in a place where there should be none, made it easy for traitors to move unseen.

I gave Representative Allston a hard look before replying. Was he in on it too?

"I can state, without reservation, that the presence of children in their high-value facilities is a deliberate tool used by their organization to protect and hide their actions from the legitimate governments in those regions. The JTTF knew inserting an operative into an adult-only compound was pointless."

You officious assclown, I concluded inaudibly before continuing aloud.

"I regret the loss of life and damage incurred. Unfortunately, it was completely unavoidable. Like all terrorist organizations these days, most of their communications are limited to in-person or physical communiqués. They use pre-digital-age technology to disseminate information to prevent hackers from infiltrating and tracking their members, most of whom have zero training and only a basic education. They eschew even the most basic augments. It is an organization full of people who are easily led and, on the surface, incapable of doing much to harm to the outside world."

"If they're incapable of doing much harm," the ambassador interrupted, "why then did the Dragon infiltrate them? Why endanger the children and destroy property?"

I turned to look at him, eager to put off going into detail about the operation itself.

"The children were in no danger. They resided in bunkers about a mile from the buildings involved."

"We're supposed to take your word for this, and the word of an agent who couldn't be bothered to appear before this committee?" He stood and tossed his digipad to the table. "I don't see why any of us should listen to this woman if she is unwilling to admit to facts we have already established, and it is an established fact that the entire compound was destroyed."

The ambassador waved his arms as if exasperated and left the platform, followed by the gazes and murmurs of displeasure from the rest of the gathered dignitaries as he pushed past them and walked swiftly down the aisle to the door. Representative Allston banged his gavel on the table in an effort to maintain decorum.

"Order! Respect the rules of the proceedings! Order!" Allston punctuated each statement with another rap of his gavel. After another few minutes, a hush descended over the crowd.

"Agent Muolo, do you deny that the compound was destroyed?"

"No, but that destruction came after the Dragon left. The Dragon was only present for the destruction of the meeting hall and armory."

"Two buildings, out of how many? And there were people in the weapons building as well, weren't there, Agent Muolo?" The ambassador's scathing voice rang through the hall from his new position by the door. I frowned but didn't take the bait.

"Ambassador, if you would like to continue to be a part of this questioning, I suggest you return to the dais and take your seat." The amplification of the speakers gave Representative Allston's voice the weight of a royal pronouncement rather than the request of a government official. I turned in my seat to look at the ambassador, almost missing the vibration behind my ear.

"Very close. Tell them now so we can confirm."

I reached up and tugged on my earlobe to activate my nonverbal response. Representative Allston looked at me shrewdly.

"Agent Muolo, why are you so certain that the destruction happened after the Dragon left?"

"The Dragon couldn't have been there because of the message."

"What message?"

"Six weeks ago, a message came into the compound. They called the leaders together so everyone could hear the message at once. The message said to cancel the op that they'd been planning on Luna. Their contact had discovered that one of the members of the cell was a spy called the Dragon. They didn't know who it was, but they knew he was within the leadership."

Several voices rose, but I pressed on.

"Only a government official could have learned that name. It was clear that we had been wrong about a corporate sponsor. This explained how they largely escaped routine sweeps by the White Hats and why their supplies seemed endless and not limited to standard weapons available on Terra. Things that could only come from someone with ties to the Unified Government, who could use IIRC resources for their own ends."

"You saw this message yourself?" Representative Allston's voice sounded strained.

I couldn't help it; I bared my teeth and leaned forward. The move would emphasize the glint of gold in my eyes, drawing attention to their exaggerated slant and size—a known side effect of eye augmentation. I searched the faces among the crowd to gauge their reactions.

"Both the messenger and the missive, because I saw everything the Dragon saw. The Dragon examined it, along with the others in the leadership of the cell, then brought it back to Luna. The PMPB leaves nothing to trust. None of them would have believed it unless they'd held it in their hands."

I took a breath and let the implications set in. I could see the light of knowledge on several faces, and I noted them. The traitor had made a mistake because the Dragon had been there for the delivery of the message—not after. The Dragon had seen the coding that had been used and had known exactly what it meant.

When I spoke again, the room was silent.

"The message was like lightning in a drought, and their tempers flared immediately. The Dragon took up position behind the man who'd brought him in, Kris Reseller, supporting him against those who thought his quick rise to power and short time with the PMPB pointed to him as the traitor. The Dragon needed him alive as Reseller ranks very high within the organization.

"In turn, Reseller accused another man, one who had come in around the same time as the Dragon—a man named Aaron Cyganovich."

"Cyganovich?" Representative Allston turned to share a look with one of the dignitaries sitting behind him, but his body blocked my view of who. I nodded.

"Despite their talk of being united in their cause, their inherent paranoia meant that they didn't trust each other in the slightest. It took only a shove to cause them to come to blows."

I took a sip of water, ignoring the slight tremor in my hands.

"It became a pitched battle between the Dragon, Reseller, and one other male and the rest, who aligned behind Cyganovich. Then someone knocked over one of the lanterns used to light the warehouse."

I shuddered, memories momentarily overtaking me. Despite my augments, despite my gifts, I was only human. It had been close, so close that I still had nightmares about it.

"Did the fire suppressant system fail?" Allston's voice barely registered, and I shook my head.

"That building. You have to understand, they didn't have

anything, nothing digital—certainly no normal fire suppression systems. The place was little more than a wooden hut with drywall plastered up in places, covered by a tin roof. It was the largest of the structures in the compound and the least modern. It was not living quarters. It might even have been a barn at one time.

"The point is, it went up like kindling. And they were too far gone to notice the world burning around them."

The room was silent now. I pressed on, eager to finish.

"The Dragon shot Cyganovich, grabbed the missive, and then dragged Reseller out the side door in the confusion. The others were making for the front. The Dragon left Reseller unconscious near the side entrance and went around to head them off. They couldn't be allowed out of there knowing about the agent." I shook my head. "Some of them never made it to the door; the smoke and flames got them. A fallen post by the main doors prevented their escape. The Dragon walked the perimeter to make sure no one slipped out one of the other entrances. No one did."

"He killed them?" Representative Allston's voice held a weight it had lacked at the start of my testimony. I didn't blame him; I'd just told everyone we'd let a dozen men and women burn to death.

"It was necessary." I put steel in my tone and raised my chin. "As was burning the armory next door. There were three remaining members of the leadership who weren't in the compound that day; those are the three who came with Reseller and the Dragon to Luna. The fire only destroyed the armory and meeting facility.

"It was the Dragon's secondary mission to ensure they didn't have any weapons capability when Terra's White Hats arrived. We didn't know they'd rigged the other buildings to explode. It was their failsafe in case the White Hats took the facility."

I looked Representative Allston in the eye, then I directly addressed the men and women siting behind him.

"They destroyed everything two days after the Dragon left, rather than let themselves be taken. Every man and woman in that compound was a traitor; they chose lives as outcasts, feeding hatred and ignorance to their children. There were few innocents in that compound and no innocents among the dead. Every one of them vowed to kill as many Augments and Syns as possible, to cleanse the system of us. They call us animals."

"Some might say burning a man alive is something an animal might do." Allston's voice sounded less confident. I scoffed.

"No, an animal would have more compassion. You forget in your outrage that these people hang and skin Augments. We infiltrated them because they weren't content to shout and spew hatred from the safety of the nets. They have attacked tourists and birthing facilities. They've killed doctors and innocents looking to get augments to cure diseases. They called down judgment when they branched out from protests to terrorism and planned the attempt on the Lunar prime minister."

I took another sip of water and scanned the assembly again. My nerves were going haywire, a clear indication something was off.

Movement at the far side of the room drew my attention. The Terran Ambassador stood in the doorway, blocking my view of the guard beside him. On the other side of the room, another pair of guards stood. One had a hand placed against his comm panel, an indication that information had come in.

I looked down at the panel on the table in front of me, then back at the guard and the bot near his feet. A flash of yellow was the only warning I got. When I heard a beep, I instinctively activated my shield.

A moment later, the dais exploded, tossing me backward like a rubber ball. I bounced off the side of the platform and onto the floor. My training took over, my muscles relaxing then tightening, allowing me to move with the force of the concussive wave and roll to my feet.

Those around me didn't fare as well. Bodies and furniture were strewn in a wide circle, the platform at its epicenter. What was left of Representative Allston lay in grisly chunks that coated every surface within five feet of the blast zone.

I turned my head toward the Terran contingent. Most of their members were awake and stampeding toward the exits. On the Lunar side, bodies lay like discarded toys in a toddler's playroom. Only a few near the back and far edge, closest to the Terrans, were mobile enough to join the throng racing for safety.

I'd suspected the PMPB might make a try for me, but I hadn't thought they would use me as a distraction for an attack.

I watched as the security forces tried to bring order to the chaos. The bots were trying to move toward the space where the explosion originated, but they were impeded by the wave of humanity struggling to get out the doors.

Amid the chaos, two figures rose, arms extended, pulse weapons gleaming in the flicker of the flames. They turned in unison, aiming in my direction.

I dove to my right and felt a hot blast of air as the beam from a pulse weapon just missed me. I rolled and came up on my knees, pulling my service weapon. Using the cover of the table, I moved in a crouched run toward the assailants.

I blocked out the sound of screams and focused on the epicenter of the explosion. I had to get there and toss my shield. The PMPB preferred dual-trigger explosives so that if the first concussion didn't succeed, the second one would.

As I approached, one assailant took aim at me. The other aimed in the direction of the Lunar delegation. And none of the security guards were close enough to be of assistance.

Timing would be everything, then.

I aimed and fired on the move, taking out the agent aiming for the delegation one-handed. With the other, I flung the shield as I executed a rolling dive designed to foul the aim of the guy trying to kill me and move us both out of the range of the small explosive device.

The agent aiming at me hadn't expected this, but his partner apparently had. Despite my shot hitting him high in the chest, he managed to fire off a blast in my direction before falling. He missed and hit his partner, sending us both tumbling closer to the delegation tables that had overturned in the explosion.

Overhead, a bit of the ceiling teetered precariously, smoke streaming off the edges, and I realized the explosion had jeopardized the integrity of the building. A single glance showed that my aim had been spot on and the shield was in place over the device. Even if they managed to trigger it remotely, it couldn't do any further damage.

A glancing impact to my leg drew my attention back to my remaining attacker. Jumping to my feet, I delivered a series of blows that he countered clumsily, his movements pained and slow from the pulse weapon wound high on his shoulder.

I stole a quick glance to where his friend lay, ensuring myself that he wasn't going anywhere. Then I knocked him out so I could move closer to the sprawl of Lunar bodies. I could see tiny movements as I neared, and I let out a sigh of relief.

Some part of me had been terrified that they'd managed to kill everyone. Moving among them, I realized that quite a few had personal shields activated. Those would have cushioned their falls and prevented impalement or the crush of falling debris. They couldn't withstand pulse or projectile weapons' fire, so the attackers had likely planned to knock everyone out with the explosion and then finish their targets off in the chaos.

I knelt, weapon at the ready, and made a visual sweep of the area around me. Two LPF officers were cuffing the unconscious assailant. They verified that the second of the two wouldn't be going anywhere ever again, then moved to clear the area around the bomb so the bots could work.

It was over. Of all the scenarios I had imagined in my endgame, a bomb had ranked low on my list of possibilities, but it had been on the list. One didn't become an IIRC officer without planning for every contingency, the more complex the better; without challenge, victory was defeat.

With a relieved sigh, I reached up and pressed the node at my neck, activating my communicator. "Well?" I asked, not needing to say more. I looked around. There were injuries and structural damage but few dead. Representative Allston had taken the brunt of the explosion.

"We traced the stream and the signal that tripped the explosion. You were right."

"I appreciate your indulgence in this, Admiral. Do you need me to accompany the team that picks them up?"

I looked around. I noted the dispersal of the fog from the fire suppressors and the gradual quieting of the room. There were only low beeps and clicks as the upkeep bots moved briskly around, clearing a path through the debris for the wounded.

"That will not be necessary. We'll handle this quietly since the ambassador may not know traitors surround him. You need only report to your commander this evening."

"Acknowledged. *Fortior concordia*, Admiral."

"*Fortior concordia*, Dragon."

One of a Kind

Jess Nickerson

6:15. 6:15. Only ten hours until 6:15.

Enya Shepard smiled to herself as her morning town car came to a stop. Taking a moment for people watching, she noticed with amusement how some let the drizzle that foretold the day's impending storm bother them into terrible moods. Even those prepared with their wellies and upturned collars seemed cross.

It's not Miami, darlings. What were you expecting?

As she stepped out onto the sidewalk, most of the passersby turned to look at her. She was dressed for the rain, of course, but not like they were. Her shoes were three-inch patent-leather booties, not flat-footed wellies. Her overcoat was not dated tweed or khaki but made from the latest fiber technology straight from Japan. Best of all, it was all in the most decadent shade of this season's "it" color: blood orange.

This moment right here, stepping from the car and rising to her full height, was one of her favorites of the day. Someone always stopped and stared, if only for an instant, and she absolutely relished it.

She looked up at the giant clock on the building's awning as if it were an ordinary day.

Only ten hours until 6:15.

The doors of the lift dinged open, and Enya breezed past the receptionist's desk. The chic woman seated behind the desk answered the phone as she watched Enya pass. "*Draped*, how can I direct your call?"

A moment later, a pretty brunette appeared, falling in step with Enya.

"Good morning, ma'am," she said, taking Enya's bag and umbrella from her.

"It certainly is, Olivia. What do we have today?"

"Morning editors' meeting in thirty, reviewing the eco-fashion spread's final layout, accessory selection for the Peggy Pennoyer shoot tomorrow, and then a free hour for reorganizing, ma'am."

"Wonderful."

Olivia took a few quick steps to pass in front of Enya and open the French doors that led into her boss's office. Enya slipped by her, stopping just inside at the coatrack to deposit her jacket. She affectionately pulled the sleeve straight as Olivia presented her with two pairs of heels to choose from for the day.

On her desk sat a steaming cup of tea and a simple but scrumptious plate of fresh fruit with golden toast. Enya listened to Olivia read off the phone messages that had come in from New York last night as she spread her marmalade, and she rolled her eyes at the requests of the American branch.

No bother. Ten hours. Only ten more hours.

"OLIVIA! Is she here yet? We've got to get her in to see—"

The thin man who had been yelling from the hall dramatically grabbed his chest. "Oh, thank God you're here! Ma'am, there's a *massive* problem with the cover. We need to start the editors' meeting now; everyone is just going absolutely *postal* about it!"

"Well, since you asked so nicely." Enya put her uneaten toast back on the plate.

"Apologies, ma'am, it's just that—"

"Roger, go tell them I'm on my way. Honestly. Olivia, gather my notes."

As they approached the conference room, Enya could hear her

colleagues yelling about photoshopping and social responsibility. She looked down at her watch.

Just nine hours and forty-five minutes now.

Seated at the long glass table, Enya listened to the back and forth for a moment.

"She feels responsible to her fans."

"Good for her! She looks fine when you're sitting and talking with her, but put this photo next to every other photoshopped magazine cover and it'll look bloody awful!"

"That's the *point*!"

"Perhaps," Enya interjected, "we can do both. A sort of before-and-after cover. Only, instead of idealizing the photoshopped version, we point out all the things we've altered. Then on the foldout, we show the untouched photo, revealing the 'true' cover."

"We do already have the charity shop spread. Maybe this could be our sort of earthy, crunchy, no-frills, express-yourself, create-your-own style, rediscover-your-own-beauty issue."

"Back to basics."

"I *love* it!"

Crisis averted, Enya listened to the other editors jabber on and list out new ideas, but she couldn't focus on their brainstorming. Her thoughts had drifted back to her own discovery of style. She had always been a fan of beautiful things and those who were able to create them.

Never having the nimble fingers to create on her own, Enya had grown up enthralled by those who had the talent and vision of true artisans. Paintings and sculptures were all well and good, but by nature, they were limiting. They had to stay on their hooks or pedestals, which made them needy. Without a fortune of her own, her younger self had had to travel to the museums and galleries that housed the masterpieces. It was time consuming, tiresome, and for someone who had just chosen to enter the working world, terribly costly. Enya hadn't been able to stand the demands that art seemed to silently make of her, but she craved their beauty.

It was then that she discovered fashion.

Her first glimpse had been a revelation. On one of her coveted museum days, she had stumbled into a traveling exhibit of vintage couture and was hooked. How had she not thought of this before? The clothes were art, and she herself could be their canvas and gallery, all in one.

Noticing a flurry of movement around her, Enya brought her thoughts back to the present. The clock at the end of the room read 11:45. She rose with the rest of them, eager to get on with the day.

6:15. 6:15. Seven hours left. Just seven hours until 6:15.

"Olivia, where are you?" Enya snapped as she stepped out of the room. "Oh, there you are. I fixed it. Within the first five minutes of my being in the room, but it wouldn't be an editors' meeting if we didn't sit there and go on and overthink every decision we've made thus far. Now, our accessory selection will have to wait. The whole shoot is going in a new direction, and it will just be a complete waste of time to attempt to foresee the path they'll blunder down next."

"Well, in that case, ma'am, we could move the reorganizing up," Olivia said.

Enya paused. "What a marvelous idea."

The two women walked back to Enya's office. This time, instead of going to sit at her desk, Enya turned the corner to the left and stood in front of a large white door with a golden handle. With her eyes closed, she stood so still, she seemed to be praying. In reality, she was just trying to calm her excitement. Finally, she reached forward and twisted the handle. For a moment, she forgot to keep counting down the minutes and just indulged in the bliss of what lay before her.

She took a step in and smiled warmly at the purses and shoes that sat on their shelves. Her hands lovingly caressed the silk scarves and luxurious fabrics of the dresses floating on hooks and hangers. Jewels of every color glistened where they rested on velvet stands, gracing the top of a specially made set of drawers. Each item had been personally collected and curated by her. Her own gallery of one-of-a-kind designer pieces. Creating a custom piece for Enya Shepard had become a milestone for ambitious aspiring designers around the globe.

"Let the reorganizing begin!" Enya said with delight. "We'll focus on the handbags, of course."

"Of course, ma'am," responded Olivia, now standing a step behind Enya. They both focused in on the shelves at the back of the closet.

Enya looked at her treasures and considered each in turn, occasionally passing one back into Olivia's waiting hands. An elegant beaded opera bag earned an extra moment of adoration as Enya grazed her fingers across the handsewn sequins.

"You know, Olivia, this is possibly the last bag that Ludwig Mercer stitched to life before his passing. It was worth a small fortune then, but now it is nearly priceless."

"It is extraordinary, ma'am. It's a shame that so often those with great talents are lost to their demons."

"Indeed, it is. Although I must admit, Olivia, there is a certain melancholic beauty to our funeral services. The world's fashion family sitting in rows, acting as macabre mannequins for our fallen kinsmen's art.

"On the other hand, the unfortunate frequency does mean they've begun to take on a certain mechanical feeling. Everyone takes a turn standing at the podium, reassuring one another that their work mattered, that their influence would be felt for generations to come. That part has become quite tedious."

Despite the tragedies that had befallen some of the designers, Enya had never felt sad looking at her collection. Instead, it brought her a proud type of peace. Having finished rearranging the purses, she simply stood in the closet, just looking at it all, not even touching anything. Sometimes that was enough, to just stand and bask in the beauty of all she had acquired.

Mine.

"Olivia, what time is it?"

"Nearly one o'clock, ma'am. Would you like me to go and fetch lunch now?"

6:15. 6:15. Just five more hours until 6:15.

"Ma'am?"

"Hmm? No, no, I'm fine, thank you."

Tonight was going to be a good night. In just over five hours, she would add a new prize to her closet. She couldn't wait. Purvis McPhee was the hottest designer of the moment. He had first entered the arena when the youngest lady of the royal family sported her very own toddler-sized purse. When her mother decided she needed one of her own, the mommy-and-me moment went viral, and suddenly he couldn't make them fast enough. That had been four months ago, and now even the little princess's poor aunties couldn't get a McPhee.

But Enya could. And tonight, she would.

McPhee was supposed to have left his atelier in Edinburgh after tea, leaving him enough time to reach *Draped* at 6:15 that evening. That was the thought that had buoyed her through the day.

6:15. 6:15. Just four more hours until 6:15.

6:15. 6:15. Just three more hours until 6:15.

It was as her own tea with Mary from advertising was beginning that Olivia walked into the room with a look of great hesitation and a note. Enya's rage and nostrils flared as she read the quick message: *McPhee's flight delayed due to storm. Will land at 8:35. Would you still like to meet here?*

Just delayed. It's still coming; it's just delayed.

"Tell him yes, we'll still meet here. Cancel my dinner with Stella. That's all."

"Of course, Enya."

8:35. 8:35. Four more hours until 8:35.

Her stomach rumbled in the basest way as she waited. It was a shame, really; the Punjabi lamb shanks from Joka were scrumptious, and she'd been looking forward to lauding her newest acquisition over Stella's head.

Two more hours until 8:35.

Unable to focus on anything beyond the ticking of the clock,

Enya found herself standing at her windows, staring into the stormy clouds to soothe herself. She had lived in the heart of London for what felt like ages now, had seen it change and grow to become what it was today, and had always been comforted by the rain. Sometimes, she believed that being constantly and consistently damp was what had allowed her to go on here for so long. Heat made tempers flare. Hers remained sated here, calmed by the cool concrete sidewalks of the city.

The dreary skies had another perk as well. Had the weather been a bit more desirable, there may have been more like her tempted to try to make the city their home. But no, her peers had opted for more fashionable and exotic cities, such as New York and Milan. Some had gone on to produce respectable work, a few had had too much fun and destroyed themselves along the way, but most had just faded into mediocrity and out of memory. This all suited Enya just fine, though an occasional jealous or unoriginal soul might imply that Enya had reached her success merely because she had so little competition.

How is that anything besides an intelligent choice? Just because I did fewer coffee runs than the rest of them, and I actually got out of the copy room. Just do your job and patch me through to the editor, sweetie.

Gossip and groan as they might, no one who knew anything could deny Enya's talent. Trends lived and died by her word. She had been single-handedly responsible for both the revival and death of the fedora in the early 2000s, and that had been in her first week as fashion editor.

She knew she had a reputation of being harsh and aloof, and normally she thoroughly enjoyed feeding into that. However, designers, like all artists, were notoriously needy, and she could not have her disdain for McPhee's faults endanger the transaction. Despite the inconvenience of the delay, she must remain welcoming enough for him to, to put it crassly, hand over the goods.

McPhee finally showed up at 10:18. Any sense of calm her mantra had provided her seemed to have left for the day with Olivia, Roger, and every other *Draped* employee. Enya could not even stand to pretend with pleasantries. He was hours late, and she did not have time to discuss how wet it was outside. She only had one purpose right then, and it was to possess her newest work of art.

"Let me see it," she said.

He made a few crass remarks about her eagerness, but her mind barely registered his immaturity. She just needed him to open the locked suitcase he was traveling with. He finally got the combination right and dramatically lifted the lid. The case was lined with quilted plum velvet, and resting serenely on top was a brown muslin lump. The thin dust bag was now the only layer between Enya and the reason she had woken up that morning. McPhee picked it up, removed that measliest of protections, and revealed his masterpiece.

It was love at first sight, and Enya was in a free fall. It was exquisite and miraculous. The curve of its handle, the U shape of its body to represent his signature horseshoe logo, and of course the color—blood orange, custom dyed. A remarkable one-of-a-kind piece, just for her.

She held it in the light and stared at it as a new grandmother would upon meeting her first grandchild. She craved every detail, soaked it all in at once, and yet it wasn't fast enough. She loved this moment more than any other. The unveiling finished, introductions complete, and now the intimate moments where she would commit every detail to her memory and store them safely in her heart. The wonderment of a new gem.

If only he would shut up.

"It's 100 percent top-grain alligator leather that we outbid Haydens for. Our dye team created this shade specifically for you. The metal is silver, melted down from serving platters bought at an estate sale in Kent intended to help pay the solicitors after a wonderfully scandalous divorce. I personally hand-tacked every corner and stitched every seam to bring this beast into creation. No other bag in our studio's history has received such attention or was born from such tantalizing materials. Hell, I haven't done one up myself since the palace called!"

McPhee's tone had been reverent as he recalled the hours spent on his masterpiece, but his ego took over and his description ended up sounding more like a reminder that Enya should be grateful he would deem her worthy of such work.

And she was, really; it was an extraordinary piece for her collection. She could not wait to carry it with her to Fashion Week.

"It really is marvelous. It's everything I was hoping for."

Enya walked into her closet and lovingly placed her new purse on the display shelf she had prepared for it. She was aware that McPhee had followed her, but while she normally reserved this space for just herself, her brain was still enjoying the bath of endorphins brought on by the purse. She didn't feel the need to spoil the moment just yet.

She could hear McPhee moving around behind her. She had expected better manners from him. A bit more awe for the art in front of him. He was, after all, standing in front of one of the finest and most expensive personal collections of jewelry in the country. Perhaps a few disbelieving exclamations over their rarity or, at the very least, how sparkly they were.

Apparently feeling quite at home, he ran his fingers over a pair of earrings. He moved on to the headpieces and picked up a quail-feather fascinator, only to unceremoniously drop it back onto the display head.

That's a fucking McQuade he just threw down, for God's sake!

It more than irked her that her collection was not being shown the proper respect. Was he on the phone now? He was on the phone! The little snot had been hours late, and now he was on the phone in her fucking closet! In front of her McQuade! She could feel her cool cracking, like the doomed earth split to reveal molten lava ready to find its way to the surface.

Just tell him to go.

"McPhee, I believe it is time for you to leave," she managed to say in a steady voice.

He acknowledged he had heard her by raising a condescending

index finger, a universally rude signal used mostly by impatient parents to pause their children. No child, Enya's eyebrows and temper both rose.

"Listen, pet, I've got to go. Love it! Yes! Paris! Amazing! Ta!" McPhee said into the phone before he pulled it from his ear and hit the red button. "Sorry, pet, what did you say?" he asked as he turned to Enya.

"I said, it is time for you to go."

"Sure, sure, gotta get your beauty rest, right, love? That's all right, no worries there. When should I come back for the interview?" McPhee's cocky smile never wavered.

"Interview?"

"Well, that's part of the deal, isn't it? That's what Lang told me, anyway. I make you something; you put me in the magazine and say I'm the new genius in town."

"That's what Lang told you, is it?"

"Well, not exactly," McPhee said. "But he said that's how he landed his first piece in one of your editorials. Figured that would be a proper payment for me as well."

"Would it now? Did Lang mention to you that after arriving on time to present me with the beautiful gift he had created for me, he literally took a step back when I first opened my closet doors? That we spent the rest of the evening discussing each piece that hangs in here? That the idea for that editorial was born of the conversation we had that day?"

Enya felt steam rising from the heat beneath the cracks. It was beginning to give her a headache.

"Uh, no, he didn't . . ."

"Lang is an artist. He understands his work is part of a larger and longer story. He lives to serve the work. He is important because his work, his art, is crucial to the continuation of the story. His work needs to be seen and shared and experienced so more people will know the story. The more people who know the story, the longer it will carry on, the longer we will all live. Do you understand what I am telling you?"

"Yeah, sure. We're artists."

"No. Lang is an artist. McQuade, who created that masterpiece you nearly knocked over moments ago, was an artist. You are a wannabe. A person with a skill and some luck. Your work, while beautiful, is not in service to the story. You do it to serve yourself. It reeks of your greed and bloated self-worth."

It felt good for Enya to lift the lid off the steam that had been building in her brain.

McPhee appeared smaller to her now. She could see what he must've looked like just a few months ago, before the young royals had inadvertently introduced him to the world.

"I thought you liked it," he barely got out.

"It is a beautiful, masterfully crafted piece," Enya replied. "It belongs in my closet. You, however, do not belong in my magazine."

She stared him down for a moment longer before he turned to go. He had been holding his phone throughout the whole humiliation, and he finally moved to put it in his pocket. As he did, something else fell from inside the cuff of his jacket. It was small, but it caught the light as it sat on the soft carpet of the office. It sparkled as it lay there, almost winking up at them.

It was a ring. It was a unique antique costume ring that had been hidden deep within the vaults of Manhattan's most famous jewelry store before it was scooped up at an auction and most lovingly placed on display in the closet. Its wide gold band was etched with curved lines, giving it a scaly effect. The blue enamel mounting was shaped to be a large reptilian skull, decorated with dozens of small clear diamonds set in a line down the center and forked into a pointed Y shape, creating horns. Completing the effect were two bright ruby eyes, on either side of the diamond snout, that shone as if they housed fire.

That's MINE!

Enya felt the fire take over inside her and did nothing to stop it. She opened her mouth as waves of heat came rippling out. Her jaw extended, dropping down to her chest, like a snake about to strike.

Enya's hands and fingers stretched to terrible lengths, her nails elongating and curving until they became talons.

With these monstrous hands, she reached out to where McPhee stood, now frozen in disbelief and terror. She wrapped her claws around his torso and legs, tilted her head back, and swiftly shoved him into her mouth and down her throat.

He didn't even have time to scream.

Enya rolled her shoulders and gave her neck a good stretch to either side as her body took on its human proportions once again. She bent down and picked up the dragon ring from the floor. She slipped it onto her finger and held her arm out, admiring the effect of the gems sparkling in the light. A satisfied smile spread across her face as she walked out of the closet and closed the door.

Moving to the coatrack, she slipped on her own trench while looking at the still wet jacket and umbrella McPhee had carried in. She picked them up and carried them with her to the elevator. She pressed the down button and waited. Another sleepy smile crept across her face as she looked around the deserted floor. Her eyes fell on the wet, ownerless items in her arms, and she silently chided herself.

I really should eat more throughout the day.

About the Authors

Charleigh Brennan lives on a sheep farm in Vermont with the permission of her dragon overlords. A San Francisco native, she is whimsical, pragmatic, and a chronic overthinker. She has studied folklore through extensive reading and her travels around the world. She likes to write about characters with diverse backgrounds who tend to be more than they appear to be. When she's not waiting for the sheep to quiet down so she can sleep or consulting her dragons on Very Important Matters, you can find her watching international movies with her Carl Jung action figure. Follow her on Facebook at Charleigh Brennan - Author.

A. R. Coble is an awkwardly pleasant fantasy writer and proud nerd-mom. Originally from Northern California, she has more than willingly called Southwest Missouri her home for more than twenty years. Andrea has a hard-working husband, two amazing daughters, and two very goofy dogs.

As a CNA working in hospice, her work is often inspired by the patients she serves. Her favorite part about working in hospice is showing her patients that they are loved while helping them maintain their dignity, even in death.

Visit her website, www.arcoble.com, and follow her on social media: on Facebook at arcoble.author, on Instagram at arcoble.author, and on Twitter at ARCoble1.

Jess Nickerson has been an educational leader and mentor for thirteen years. Inspired by stories she read in class to her students, she began writing her own. When she isn't teaching or writing, she can be found hunting down treasures at thrift shops or overthinking things at the grocery store. She has a double BA in Literature and Elementary Education and is a certified floral designer. She lives in Massachusetts with her husband and their two cats. This is her first published piece. You can claim you've been a fan since before she was big by following her on Instagram at storytime_jess.

D. Gabrielle Jensen is an artist of many media, but words have always been her strongest passion. A traditional bachelor's degree in English and Creative Writing from Colorado State University–Pueblo led to more than a decade as a freelance web content creator, music reviewer, and author for a variety of publications, including an eight-year stint as owner and chief editor of a speculative fiction magazine and the self-publication of two collections of poetry, *Frenetic Lines* and *Battle Magic.*

When she is not writing, she is bringing art to the world through cosmetology, jewelry design, photography, and the occasional spare pencil sketch. Music drifts into every aspect of her life, and even though she doesn't create it, it is always playing, always inspiring. She is an extrovert and loves people, so join her adventures on Facebook at D. Gabrielle Jensen, on Instagram at writerdgabrielle, and on Twitter at dgabrielejensen, or support her on Patreon (www.patreon.com/writerdgabrielle). And don't forget to say hi.

G. Pearl Kilgore has been a sci-fi fan since childhood and enjoys writing speculative fiction. *Dragons Within* is her second anthology. She was a finalist in the 2018 Stories of the Nature of Cities 2099 writing competition, and her short story entry, "Contraband," was featured in *A Flash of Silver Green: Stories of the Nature of Cities* by Publication Studios. She is currently writing her first novel. She enjoys exploring contemporary issues in her work, such as disability advocacy, medical ethics, environmental concerns, and civil rights. She has degrees in Allied Health Management and Early Childhood Development and has worked in both healthcare and education. She has a passion for science that she shares with her four children. She has two lazy cats but would love to have a pet dragon. Her son says that's not a good idea, though, because it may eat the pet unicorn that he hopes to one day create in a lab.

C. M. Lander is an emerging voice in the fantasy and science fiction genres. She holds a bachelor's degree in Creative Writing from Hofstra University, where she focused on her first love: poetry. She published her first novella, *Friendless*, in 2018, and her short stories have appeared in *Beyond the Mask: A Fiction-Atlas Superhero Anthology* and Seacrest Publishing's *Cirque de Vol Mystique*. She has been featured as Tumblr's Poet of the Day and placed second in the Bartleby Snopes Dialogue Only Contest.

C. M. is currently a student of law and is devoted to marrying her love of writing with philanthropic causes.

Allorianna Matsourani grew up on the East Coast of the United States near Annapolis, Maryland, and has been a writer at heart since she wrote her first fantasy short story at age twelve. She attended journalism school at the University of Maryland and has directed her writing efforts toward nonfiction articles for newspapers and magazines. Most recently, Allorianna was the editor of a business-to-business magazine for the oil and gas, chemical, water and wastewater, coatings, marine, and power generation industries.

An avid reader and fan of science fiction, fantasy, and mystery novels, Allorianna has spent the past several years refocusing her writing on fiction. "The Power of the Sword" is her second short story to appear in an anthology.

JT Morse is a speculative fiction writer of emotional poetry and character-driven narratives. She's had work published in the *Creatives Rising* e-zine, the *Animal Uprising!* horror anthology from Nightmare Press, and other literary publications under the pen name JT Haven. You can find her on social media as JTMorseAuthor.

Amanda Salmon is a young adult fantasy author. She loves magic and the supernatural. She has even gone ghost hunting. Fortunately, she never encountered a real specter; unlike her characters, she has not been gifted with magical abilities.

Amanda lives in a small town in Kentucky, where she finds inspiration all around her. The donkeys across the road have been extremely helpful at the most inconvenient times with their banshee wails.

You can follow her on Facebook at Amanda Salmon - Author.

K. T. Seto writes short stories and novels—which you probably figured out since you're super smart and awesome. They're mostly speculative fiction and paranormal romance, so don't go looking for damsels in distress or the next Tolstoy in any of her works. They're strictly a way to escape for a few hours in your favorite chair with the accompaniment of your choice. Wine? Cookies? The blood of your enemies? Whatever.

K. T. also has a deep and abiding love of chocolate—like most people fortunate enough to have tasted it (unless they're allergic or sociopathic)—and a compulsion to play what-if. Look for news of her work on social media: KatAboutThat on Instagram and K.T.Seto- Author on Facebook. Her website is coming, summer 2019.

Dorothy Tinker makes weird work! With a love of the literary and a fondness for numbers, she spins connections between her readers and the worlds she writes with a depth and complexity that will leave you wanting more.

Dorothy writes stories focused on the spiritual and fantastical. She has three award-winning books published in her Peace of Evon series. Her short stories range through fantasy, science fiction, and suspense and can be found in anthologies published by Inklings Publishing, Writespace, HWG Press, and Balance of Seven.

You can follow Dorothy on Facebook at Dorothy Tinker - Author or on Twitter at dorothy_tinker or dtinker_editing. Connect with her more deeply by becoming a magical creature in her Weirdly Whimsical World at www.patreon.com/DorothyTinker.

E. A. Williams is a writer of many genres. Her interests focus on gothic literature, as well as crime and paranormal romance.

Her work will capture your raw emotions, bringing you into a world of suspense and exposing you to sheer terror.

Combining her medical background and vivid imagination, as well as hobbies that include culinary creations and art, she explores many avenues to bring her writing to life.

E. A. Williams is a California native currently residing in Texas with her husband and daughters. You can follow her on: Facebook at Writer E.A. Williams, Instagram at writer_e.a.williams, and Twitter at WriteEAWilliams.

CPSIA information can be obtained
at www.ICGtesting.com
Printed in the USA
FFHW011223130819
54211394-59941FF